William Stokes

**William Stokes**

his life and work - 1804-1878

William Stokes

**William Stokes**
*his life and work - 1804-1878*

ISBN/EAN: 9783337423674

Printed in Europe, USA, Canada, Australia, Japan

Cover: Foto ©Andreas Hilbeck / pixelio.de

More available books at **www.hansebooks.com**

# WILLIAM STOKES

## His Life and Work

## (1804—1878)

BY HIS SON

## WILLIAM STOKES

SURGEON-IN-ORDINARY TO THE QUEEN IN IRELAND

"His life was gentle, and the elements
So mixed in him that Nature might stand up
And say to all the world, 'This was a man.'"

*NEW YORK*
LONGMANS, GREEN & CO.
91 & 93 FIFTH AVENUE
1898

To

MARGARET McNAIR STOKES

THE BELOVED DAUGHTER AND CONSTANT

COMPANION OF HIM WHOSE LIFE MUST EVER SERVE

AS A BEACON TO THOSE WHO STRIVE TO ELE-

VATE THE PROFESSION OF MEDICINE,

THIS WORK IS DEDICATED

BY HER BROTHER

THE AUTHOR

# PREFACE

IN presenting this Memoir the writer, being to a great extent at a disadvantage, as a son must always be who attempts a biography of his father, hopes that his effort will be regarded with indulgence by the reader. His object has been to convey the impression of the wide sympathies, many-sided nature, and greatness of the character pourtrayed, not so much by description, as by a simple record of the scientific work achieved by him, along with what may be gathered from his addresses and occasional letters, of his exalted standard of professional honour, and his love and appreciation of the beautiful in Nature and Art.

Apart from the interest that is always attached to the history of the lives of those who have distinguished themselves in literature, science, or art, much may be gained by such study in affording indications as to the methods to follow and the pitfalls to avoid in our efforts to effect advancement in any of these branches of knowledge. In the present day, when so much difference of opinion exists as to the most desirable system of medical education, it seems specially important to note how those who have most deeply impressed their names on the annals of medicine worked as students, and how the methods of study pursued by them, which would now be considered so defective, were followed by such brilliant results. Certain it is, that no two systems of education could differ more than the one which existed during the pupilage of Hunter, Brodie, Cooper, Graves, and other Masters of Medicine, and that which exists at the present day. And what may be said of the education of these pioneers of medical and surgical science, applies also to that in connection with other branches of human knowledge, as already acknowledged in the case of the Fine Arts.

In drawing attention to this, the writer's object is not to advocate a return to the old educational methods, but to point out that they had one great merit in which the existing system is deficient,

namely, the large opportunities they afforded for culti-
vating the faculty of original observation ; students
formerly had more time and far greater facilities
for pursuing the special branches of science ancillary
to medicine for which individually they had particular
aptitude and taste. Now a Procrustean educational
path, bristling with topics, most of which should be
relegated to post-graduate study, is laid down, which
all students, irrespective of their tastes and abilities,
must follow, and the results in most instances are
superficiality and inaccuracy, the reverse of what
was anticipated by our modern educational reformers.
I would commend to them the words of the wise
and true statement of Professor Baynes, " It is not at
school, but by his own self-imposed studies afterwards,
that a man is educated."

I have endeavoured in the following pages to give
not only what is necessarily a brief account of my
father's scientific work, and the additions made by
him to our knowledge, but also by dwelling on his
home pursuits, his tastes, and accomplishments to
furnish to some extent a picture of his *inneres Leben* ;
and, by a few selected anecdotes illustrative of Irish
pathos and humour, to give an idea of some characteristics of the people among whom he lived and

worked, and of the country that gave him birth, and that he loved so well.

For many valuable suggestions my warm acknowledgments are due to my sister Miss Margaret Stokes, to Sir Henry Acland, Bart., Sir William Gairdner, K.C.B., Dr. Arthur Wynne Foot, Dr. J. W. Moore, and finally Dr. Samuel Gordon, one of my father's most trusted friends and advisers.

To Miss Blanche Bellasis my warm acknowledgments are also due for the great trouble she has taken in the preparation of the index.

# CONTENTS

B

# CONTENTS

## CHAPTER VIII.

## CHAPTER IX.

## CHAPTER X.

## CHAPTER XI.

## CHAPTER XII.

## CHAPTER XIII.

---

# ILLUSTRATIONS

# WILLIAM STOKES

---

## I

## LINEAGE, BIRTH, AND EARLY STUDENT LIFE

WILLIAM STOKES, the subject of this Memoir, belonged to a family, members of which have for five generations occupied more or less prominent positions in the public life of Ireland. Gabriel Stokes, the first of his forefathers who settled in Ireland, was an engineer by profession, and became Deputy Surveyor-General. He came to Dublin about the year 1680, and appears to have resided there the greater part of his life. The similarity of his arms, family tradition and a seal, impressions of which exist, and which he bequeathed to his son John, on which is engraved his crest and arms, indicate that he probably belonged to a junior branch of the Stokes family long resident in Gloucestershire. Of this family, Sir Bernard

Burke has recorded that it was of Norman origin, and "it appears that its ancestors must have come to England after the Conquest, when houses and possessions were assigned to them. Their history, however, is not uninterruptedly traced until the time of Edward II., 1312, when we find by records in the Tower, that Sir Adam de Stocke was seized of the Manors of Stokke and Rutishall in the county of Wilts. Thomas, his eldest son, held the manor of Seende, with other lands in Wiltshire, and Roger, his second son, the manors of Wolfshall Savernagge and Hungerford, in the same county. The latter (Roger) with his father, Sir Adam, were interred in the church of Great Bedwyn, to which they had been benefactors, where their monuments and effigies are still to be seen. John, a descendant of Thomas, represented the county in parliament in the time of Charles II. In the reign of Elizabeth we find John Stokys (the first change which took place in the orthography of the name) erected the chapel or church of Seende, and is interred there. In the fifteenth century Christopher Stokes (when the name finally changed), held the manor of Stanishawes and Codrington, with other lands in the same county, and about 1700, Richard Stokes, of Calne Castle, in Wiltshire, held considerable possessions in the counties of Gloucester and Berks " (" Landed Gentry of Great Britain," 1847, p. 1308).

In the "Historical Memorials of Canterbury," by the late Dean Stanley, we learn that Aleyn de Stocke was one of the executors of the will of Edward the Black Prince, and it appears in the Register of William (Courtenay) Archbishop of Canterbury, 1386, that Aleyn de Stocke and John Bishop of Durham "had rendered their account of the goods and had a full acquittance," and also another acquittance from the Prior and Chapter of Christ Church, Canterbury, for the legacies bequeathed to that church by the Prince.

When Gabriel Stokes was resident in Dublin (1680–1721) he there published various works on Engineering, including " A scheme for effectually supplying every part of the City of Dublin with pipe water without any charge for water engines or any water forcers, by a close adherence to the laws of gravitation and the principles, rules, and experiments of Hydrostaticks." He was also the author of " The Mathematicians Cabinet of the Hydrostatist Balance unlocked ; or an Easy Key to all its Uses." In the Record Office, in Dublin, there are a considerable number of maps of various districts in Ireland countersigned by him, and being an engineer of much reputation, he was employed by the Government in various public works for the improvement of the Port of Dublin, among others the Great Pigeon House Wall, which protects the south side of the entrance into the Liffey. He obtained official recognition of these services in 1721, when he was accorded a forestaff as a crest by William Hawkins, Ulster, "for his skill in his profession." This was during the Viceroyalty of His Grace the Duke of Grafton.

Gabriel Stokes had two sons, John, born 1716, and Gabriel, born 1726, both of whom were Scholars and Fellows of Trinity College. The former was Regius Professor of Greek and Archbishop King's Lecturer. He ultimately obtained a College living in the County Donegal, where he settled. He was a classical scholar of much repute, and published an edition of Demosthenes. His son was the father of Sir George Gabriel Stokes, Bart., F.R.S., late President of the Royal Society, and of the late Rev. J. W. Stokes, Archdeacon of Armagh. The second son Gabriel, became Professor of Mathematics, and like his brother, eventually took a College living, and settled in Waterford where he was Chancellor of

Waterford Cathedral.[1] He edited Hippolytus and Iphigenia in Aulis, and was author of an Essay on Newcome's "Harmony of the Gospels," and one on Subscription to the Thirty-Nine Articles. His eldest son Whitley, born 1763, was the father of the subject of the present memoir.

Whitley Stokes, like his father and uncle, was a Scholar and Senior Fellow of Trinity College, and held a position of great prominence in the scientific, literary, and political circles in the Irish capital towards the end of the last and beginning of the present century. He was a man of pure and lofty aims, singular unselfishness, untiring energy, and capable of such self-devotion as too often frustrates its own object. In the pursuit of means by which he might promote the moral interests and physical resources of his country all else was forgotten. In early life it was his intention to take Holy Orders, but, on obtaining a fellowship in Trinity College, he relinquished that idea, and

[1] In connection with the much disputed point as to whether the marriage of Dean Swift with Hester Johnson (Stella) ever took place, the writer may mention that his aunt, Miss Ellen Stokes, now many years deceased, stated that her grandfather informed her that the Bishop of Clogher, who was an intimate friend of Swift, and also of Gabriel Stokes, told the latter that the ceremony had taken place in the Dean's garden—now the site of the Meath Hospital—and that he himself had officiated.

devoted himself to the study of medicine. About the year 1800 he became Professor of the Practice of Medicine in the Royal College of Surgeons, which Chair he held for several years. In the year 1816, having become a Non-Conformist, he felt compelled to resign his Senior Fellowship. His services, however, were not lost to the University, as he was appointed to the Lectureship on Natural History, and ultimately was elected Regius Professor of Medicine. In early life he became a member of the Society of United Irishmen, in the first months of its existence, but as soon as he found that the object of its associates was not to be confined to effecting reforms by peaceful and constitutional means, he retired from taking any action in their proceedings. This was in 1792. However, it being suspected that his sympathies were still largely with the movement, and the principles advocated by Grattan, Curran, and other Irish patriots and friends, he was cited to appear before the Vice-Chancellor of the University, Lord Clare, with the result that, notwithstanding his previous secession from the society, and before it had become a secret organisation, he was suspended from his Fellowship for a year. In abandoning the society, he did not lose the esteem of one, at all events, of its most prominent members, viz., Theobald Wolfe Tone, who wrote of him, " We, however, differed on many material points and we differ on principles which do honour to Stokes' heart. With an acute feeling of the degradation of his country and a just and generous indignation against her oppressors, the tenderness and humanity of his disposition is such that he recoils from any measure to be attempted for her emancipation which may terminate in blood. In this respect I have not the virtue to imitate him. I must observe that with this perhaps extravagant anxiety for the lives of others, I am sure that in any case that satisfied his conscience, no man would be more prodigal of his own life than Whitley Stokes, for he is an enthusiast in his nature, but what he would highly, that would he holily, and I am afraid in the present state of affairs that is a thing impossible. I love Stokes most sincerely. With a most excellent and highly cultivated mind he possesses the distinguishing characteristic of the best and most feeling heart, and I am sure that it will not hurt the self-love of any of the friends whose names I have recorded when I say in the full force of the phrase, that I look upon Whitley Stokes as the very best man I have ever known."

An interesting account of this "Visitation" of 1798 is given in Dr. Stubbs' "History of the University of Dublin, from 1591 to 1800." "Whitley Stokes, when questioned by the Vice-Chancellor, denied that he knew of the existence of societies of United Irishmen in the College, or of any illegal or secret societies within the walls. He admitted that he had been a member of the Society of United Irishmen in 1791, before their revolutionary tendencies had been developed; but he stated that from that period he had altogether dissociated himself from them. He admitted that he had occasionally visited as a physician a man who was well known for his treasonable proclivities, but who was very ill and very poor. He was always accompanied by a third person, lest his action might be misrepresented. He had also subscribed to a fund which was formed to relieve the necessities of two members of the United Irishmen who were in prison. The most reliable evidence was given on Dr. Stokes' behalf, that he had used his influence, which was considerable, with the students to induce some of them to withdraw from treasonable associations, and to enrol their names among the members of the College Corps, and that his efforts had been successful." [1] Notwithstanding this testimony, the visitors decided that in consequence of his having confessed that he had had intercourse with leaders of the conspiracy, he should be precluded from acting as college tutor, should for three years be disqualified from sitting as a member of the Board, and from being co-opted to a Senior Fellowship. The sentence was confirmed by the Duke of Gloucester, as Chancellor of the University, in May, 1798. The decision was considered a very harsh one, and " those who knew the integrity of Dr. Stokes' character, and the kindliness of heart and humanity by which he was marked, could not believe that the sentence which Lord Clare and Dr. Duigenan had passed upon him was justified. We must remember that both the visitors were men of strong party feeling, and that Stokes as well as Brown, entertained extreme liberal views in politics, while they were both thoroughly opposed to seditious and disloyal proceedings."

To various branches of natural history, especially botany, zoology, mineralogy, and chemistry, and to the development of the industrial resources of

---

[1] "The History of the University of Dublin, from its foundation to the end of the Eighteenth Century," by John William Stubbs, D.D., S.F.T.C.D. 1889. p. 298.

Ireland, he now devoted himself with characteristic enthusiasm. He took an active part in the
arrangement and foundation of the College
Botanical Gardens, and was one of the founders
of the Zoological Gardens in the Phœnix Park.
As a proof of his many-sided nature and wide
sympathies it may be mentioned that he published
at his own expense a translation of the New
Testament into Irish, and in conjunction with
the Rev. B. Mathias, and the Rev. W. Stephens,
originated the Irish Society. Although he devoted
so much time to the pursuit of natural science,
politics, and literature, he was not, as Sir Charles
Cameron has pointed out in his excellent memoir,[1]
unmindful of his functions as a physician and "was
ever ready to minister to the wants of the sick
poor." He worked hard during the epidemic of
typhus fever, and in a treatise on contagion, he
strongly advocated the isolation of the sick, the
purification of their dwellings and clothing, and
the establishment of district hospitals.[2]

[1] "History of the Royal College of Surgeons," by Sir Charles A.
Cameron, 1886.
[2] The following is a list of some of his published writings :—" Essay
on Respiration," 1793. "Observations on Contagion," two Editions.
"Observations on the Necessity of publishing the Scriptures in the Irish

In his home life, his tastes, being distinctly artistic, he encouraged these in his children, some of whom, especially in painting, gave promise of great future distinction. To music, poetry, and painting, he was perhaps as devoted as he was to any of the many branches of natural science, in the pursuit of which he made for himself so lasting a reputation. He died at the advanced age of eighty-two on April 13, 1845.[1]

Whitley Stokes numbered among his friends some of the most brilliant men of the day, when social life in Dublin was remarkable for the genius, wit, and grace that shone at its friendly gatherings. It is related that on one evening at a dinner party at his house in Harcourt Street were met together Charles Kendal Bushe, the most graceful and attractive of speakers; William C. Plunket, subsequently Lord Chancellor of Ireland, the last of the remarkable group of orators in the closing half of the eighteenth century; John Philpot Curran, whose

Language." A prize Essay in reply to Paine's "Age of Reason." Letters in reply to Part II. of Paine's "Age of Reason." "Observations on the Population and Resources of Ireland in reply to Malthus," &c.

[1] Mr. Lecky refers more than once to the writings of Whitley Stokes, "whose tracts," he says, "throw much light upon the agrarian history of his time in Ireland" ("Ireland in the Eighteenth Century," vol. iii. pp. 409, 412-14).

bright genius has been compared to a prism " catching
the radiance that shone around him, breaking into a
thousand hues of rainbow colour "; William Magee,
distinguished as an author and divine, then Professor
of Mathematics in Trinity College, afterwards Archbishop of Dublin ; and Peter Burrowes, the eloquent
lawyer, whose speeches in the Irish Parliament were
models of clear and forcible reasoning.    These and
other distinguished men were gathered round the table,
when a question was started as to what constituted the
chief qualification of a delightful companion and friend,
upon which matter it was sportively agreed that
each person should deliver his opinion in succession.
One said it consisted of wit ; another of humour ; a
third, a combination of both ; a fourth, of learning
readily producible upon any occasion that might be
started ; a fifth, a powerful memory stored with
anecdote ; a sixth, of sound philosophical views ; when
Mr. Burrowes cried out, " Are you all done ? "
and when all eyes turned towards him he electri-
fied them by striking the table with his fist and
saying, " It is Honesty by G——"

William Stokes, the subject of this memoir, was
the second son of Whitley Stokes, and was born
in Dublin, July, 1804. His earliest years were

spent at his father's country-house, Ballinteer, in the Dublin hills. As a boy he did not give indications of exceptional ability, and was apparently by nature indolent and apathetic as regards both physical and intellectual effort. He had no aptitude for games, field sports, or athletics ; but at an early age he exhibited a love for poetry and romance which in after life he never lost. It is narrated of him that when still a boy a favourite habit of his was to retire to what he termed his " nest " which he had made in a thick beech hedge and there he studied, and committed to memory, many of the Scottish Border Ballads, which a short time previously had been published by Sir Walter Scott. These tales of heroism, devotion, love, and revenge had for the boy an absorbing interest and fascination, not less than that he afterwards experienced from reading the Waverley novels, works which, throughout his whole life, and almost to the day of his death, were sources of the keenest pleasure to him.

The desultory studies to which Stokes in his early youth was so much devoted, and his indolence in carrying out any steady methodical system of study, were sources of real concern to his parents, and caused his mother, especially, much anxious thought. One day, while in his favourite retreat, he fell asleep, but shortly afterwards was awakened by some warm drops falling on his face. He started up and saw his mother bending over him. Her tears had awakened him. Stung with remorse at having been a cause of so much sorrow, his nature appeared to undergo an immediate and salutary change, and the dreamy indolent boy suddenly became the ardent enthusiastic student. The influence of Whitley Stokes' character and the intellectual atmosphere he created around him, could not fail to foster and develop the mental power of his son who now became assistant in his father's laboratory, and a constant companion during his frequent rambles among the hills and valleys of Dublin and Wicklow, studying practical botany, geology, and mineralogy. In these walks, too, he doubtless became embued with that passionate love for the external beauties of nature which throughout his life was one of his keenest pleasures. He had also the advantage of meeting occasionally his father's distinguished friends, among whom were some of the brightest intellects of the day, such men as those already mentioned as well as Henry Grattan, James

Martineau; O'Conor, the landscape painter; J. Parsons, the eminent lawyer; and Petrie, the archæologist, and accomplished musician and artist. Such advantages as these to a large extent compensated for the want of the methodical school and collegiate education the benefits of which were denied to William Stokes, owing to the peculiar views on the subject of education held by his father, who over-estimated the advantages, moral and physical, to be derived from home education.

The mixed condition of society in Dublin at this period is difficult now to realise—so strong was the contrast between such brilliant intellects as those of the friends Whitley Stokes gathered round him, and the ill-ordered and indolent character prevalent in the mass of the Irish nation immediately after the Union. On one side brilliant talent, energy, humour, sparkling fun, refinement, and poetry; on the other dejection, discontent, inertness, or, more mournful still than all, indifference to aught but selfish and petty intrigue. If we would know somewhat of the labours of those who strove for better things, we must not ignore the difficulties that thus met them on every side in that land for which, to use the words of Whitley Stokes, "God had done so much and man so little."

It must not however be supposed that in William Stokes' early education classics and mathematics were altogether neglected, for he had for many years as tutor the well-known scholar and mathematician, John Walker, F.T.C.D., a learned author, whose edition of Livy was published in 1777, and also of Euclid, a work still in use. From this teacher he learned Greek, Latin, and mathematics. It was to him always a source of profound regret in after life that he had not been allowed to enter college, since no one ever more fully realised the importance of university training and education. However, in his instance the loss, as already pointed out, was largely compensated. His education commenced in boyhood at his father's side, from whom he derived that taste and aptitude for physical science to which, while a student, he he devoted himself with unceasing industry and enthusiasm. Chemistry appears at this period to have had special attraction for him, and this doubtless was largely due to his intimacy with, and warm friendship for, James Apjohn, who subsequently became celebrated as a teacher and investigator in that science.

After studying Clinical Medicine for some time in the Meath Hospital, and the sciences, ancillary to medicine, especially that of chemistry, in the laboratory of

Trinity College and the Royal College of Surgeons, he went to Glasgow, where for fully two years he again worked mainly at chemistry in the laboratory and under the direction of Professor Thompson. He then, acting on his father's advice, proceeded to Edinburgh to complete the studies required for a medical degree which he hoped to obtain there. Here it was that, stimulated by the magnetic influence of Professor Alison, he developed that study for Clinical Medicine and that rare power of original observation and research which enabled him at an early age to take so prominent and foremost a place among the pioneers of medical science. The account of his first interview with Alison is thus graphically given by Sir Henry Acland in his admirable biographical sketch of William Stokes.[1] "He was walking one wet night down the old Cowgate; he observed a crowd at the entrance of a dark passage; he stopped to see what it could mean; he entered a low room filled with sick poor, Professor Alison being seated among them; he watched the scene; a young man evidently suffering from advanced fever stepped forward. Alison said, 'Go

[1] "William Stokes." A Sketch drawn for the New Sydenham Society, by Henry W. Acland, Regius Prof. of Medicine in the University of Oxford. London, 1882.

31

to your bed and when I have done here I will come to you.' Young Stokes then stepped forward and said, 'Sir, I will take the poor man to his home.' 'Who are you?' asked Alison. 'One of your pupils; my name is Stokes.' 'I never saw you before,' said Alison. 'Perhaps not, but I have seen you, for I go to your lectures. Let me take the poor man home and I will come and tell you how he goes on.' 'Very well,' said Alison, 'you may go.' From that time they were companions and friends."

Later in life William Stokes observed of his great teacher, "Alison was the best man I ever knew. I wonder how it has happened that men should forget what reverence is due to his memory—whether we look on him personally as a man of science and a teacher, or at his life as that of an exemplar of a soldier of Christ. It was my good fortune to be very closely connected with him during my student days in Edinburgh, and to attend him by day and more often far into the night in his visits of mercy to the sick poor of that city to whom he was for many a year physician, friend, and support."

From nine at night to two or three o'clock in the morning we seem to see this wise and good physician attended by William Stokes, the ardent youth of twenty-one years of age, as full of love for his great teacher as of zeal for his art, passing through snow and storm down the Cowgate and up the high stairs leading to the topmost flat on some old house in the wynds of Edinburgh, bringing medicine and healing to the dark haunts of poverty and misery, comfort and sympathy to the wounded souls at whose bedside they ministered.

About this time the profession was much exercised by the great advance made in the French School more particularly in the power of diagnosis of thoracic diseases through the advocacy of auscultation and percussion by Laennec. Like many other innovations and discoveries in medicine and surgery, it was long before the methods were recognised as reliable adjuvants in the art of diagnosis. But William Stokes at once grasped the importance and far-reaching results which he saw would ensue from Laennec's great discovery. Accordingly, and before he obtained any medical qualification, he prepared and published in Edinburgh in 1825 a small treatise on the use of the stethoscope, for which work he received the sum of £70.[1] This work, followed in 1828 by the publication

[1] Although Dr. Cullen, to whom Stokes dedicated his work, and Sir J. Forbes both published cases illustrative of the practical use of the stethoscope in the diagnosis of thoracic disease, to Stokes is unquestion-

of two lectures on the application of the stethoscope to the diagnosis and treatment of thoracic disease, may be said to be the foundation stones of the great super-structure, namely, his treatise on diseases of the chest, which appeared eleven years afterwards, and which was the work on which his reputation and fame may be said mainly to rest.

In reference to the two lectures above referred to, the author of a short sketch of William Stokes which appeared in the *Dublin University Magazine*, August, 1874, observes : " The importance of these lectures at the time they were delivered to the class of the Meath Hospital cannot be overrated. The science of the stethoscope was then only in its infancy, and like everything else that is new, no matter how valuable it may be, was met with opposition and adverse criticism by those who either would not or, from their own deficiencies, could not appreciate its value. Not so with Dr. Stokes, his medical mind saw in the simple instrument that was spurned and despised by others a new and powerful weapon to aid him in the great battle with disease and death."

ably due the credit of publishing the first systematic treatise in the English language on the subject. The date of the publication is 1825.

In the first of these lectures he says, "The sense of hearing has been called to our assistance and has, I will affirm, added more to the facility, certainty, and utility of diagnosis than anything that has been done for centuries." Twelve years later he wrote, "Time has already shown that the introduction of auscultation and its subsidiary physical signs has been one of the greatest boons ever conferred by the genius of man on the world. A new era in medicine has been marked by a new science depending on the immutable laws of physical phenomena, and, like other discoveries founded on such a basis, simple in its application and easily understood. A gift from science to a favoured son, not as was formerly supposed, a means of merely forming a useless diagnosis in incurable disease, but one by which the ear is converted into the eye, the hidden recesses of visceral disease opened to the view, a new guide in the treatment and a new help in the early detection, prevention, and cure of the most widely-spread diseases which affect mankind."[1]

As an illustration of how long it takes for the adoption of any novelty in practice, no matter how

[1] "A Treatise on the Diagnosis and Treatment of Diseases of the Chest," pp. 40, 41, Dublin, 1837.

high its credentials, a statement made by Sir Henry Acland, one of William Stokes' best and most constant friends, with reference to the great use of the stethoscope, may·he mentioned : "I cannot but remember now that more than ten years after this passage was written, I myself being a clerk in a great hospital, had to withstand the ridicule of an able teacher for devoting myself to the mastery of the instrument."

## II

PROFESSIONAL LIFE IN DUBLIN—ROBERT GRAVES—
CLINICAL TEACHING—THE MEATH HOSPITAL
—EPIDEMIC OF TYPHUS FEVER—MARRIAGE

IN the autumn of 1825 Stokes having obtained his
degree in Edinburgh, returned to Dublin and
shortly after was elected to his first professional
appointment, Physician to the Dublin General Dispensary. Though no direct emolument was attached
to the office yet it was an honourable one, involving
great labour, and was eventually of essential service to
him as an introduction to practice. Writing at this
time to the lady who subsequently became his wife,
he observed : " In the course of my practice here I
meet with instances of want and wretchedness that
wring my very heart, and I wish for the fortune of a
prince that I might relieve them. Charity is of all

virtues the fairest and most boundless and sometimes even here meets its reward. One gentleman whose vote I came to solicit said, 'I will vote for you, sir, for the sake of your father, who thirty-two years ago brought a bottle of wine in his pocket to an unfortunate man who lived behind my house.' This was 'bread thrown on the waters' which I found 'after many days.'"

In 1826 after many months of laborious dispensary work, one of the offices of Physician to the Meath Hospital becoming vacant owing to Dr. Whitley Stokes' resignation, William Stokes was elected in his place, the reputation he had obtained on the publication of his treatise on the use of the stethoscope, having doubtless largely contributed to his success at the election. Feeling the necessity for some rest and change before commencing his clinical work at the hospital, he set out with a few friends for North Wales, among the mountains and valleys of which he spent a short but pleasant holiday. The following extract from one of his letters at this time gives a fair idea of his exceptional power of word painting :—

"*Aug.* 15, 1826.—Our next day's march was through the delightful valley leading to Snowdon, which mountain we ascended. I do not think the

38

view as beautiful from its top as that from Ben Lomond, but it is stupendous. Enormous excavations crowned by rugged peaks yawn in every direction round the spectator, and make one think that here was the focus of some of Nature's wildest convulsions. Our next day was spent fishing in the lakes through the romantic valley of Beddgelert—sometimes ascending the mountains to mineralogise or botanise. I think you would have laughed to have seen me with a fishing basket on my back, an angling rod in my hand, and a Shakespeare peeping out of my breast pocket. On that evening we saw a beautiful phenomenon. The sun was setting behind one of the peaks of Snowdon while a huge mass of white cloud poured down from the adjoining hill into its deep excavation, but the curious circumstance was that as soon as the rays of the sun shot across this body of vapour it instantly ascended, coming up the precipice like a pillar of flame and giving the idea of a volcano in its proudest action. I remained more than half an hour gazing on the scene in silent admiration."

On his return he commenced his clinical work at the Meath Hospital, where he had the great advantage of having as a loyal colleague the illustrious Robert

James Graves, who became his life-long friend. From his rare erudition, the variety of his mental powers, his industry, and the additions which he made to practical medicine, he was, in William Stokes' opinion, the most remarkable man of which the profession in this country can boast. To be associated with one so richly endowed with intellectual power, combined with an almost boyish simplicity of character, who was mentally humble but naturally proud, was Stokes' rare good fortune.

For years they worked together in the Meath Hospital, assisting one another in their clinical researches, and in the initiation and carrying out of a system of clinical instruction till then unknown in this country, which eventually acquired a world-wide fame for the Dublin School of Medicine. Never did any disagreement arise between them. In such natures envy and jealousy had no place, and the lapse of time only strengthened and cemented the bonds between them of friendship, loyalty, and affection.

The success of Stokes' early researches, as well as the brilliant reputation acquired by M. Andral in the French School of Medicine by his labours in the same field, may be attributed to two causes. Stokes and Andral both had a careful preliminary training in many of those sciences which are ancillary to medicine, and with the undaunted energy and enthusiasm or youth they were enabled to carry their knowledge and abilities to the bedside of the patient and apply them to the elucidation of the phenomena of disease. Their works would probably never have seen the light had these opportunities been denied them, and, as has been well said, " They afford proof of the advantages accruing to science from placing young men of talent and education in a fair field of observation and experience at an early age. Had such opportunities been withheld in the case of the authors in question, even for a few years, the result would probably have been what we continually see in the appointments to great hospitals in this country. The most competent men have to wait in 'hope deferred' year after year, until at last, when haply they do gain the object of their wishes, their ardour is gone, much of their knowledge and habit of study lost through disuse, their minds are contracted by the limits of some petty and imperfect sphere of observation to which circumstances have confined them, and last, not least, the *res angusta domi* has rendered the engagements of a scanty private practice, or of any other more *direct* way of getting a livelihood, of more pressing importance than working for the science, or for the ultimate improvement of the art, of medicine."[1]

After his appointment to the Meath Hospital the first task which Stokes undertook, aided by his colleague Graves, was to effect a salutary and much needed reform in the system of clinical teaching. Up to his time practically no real attempt had been made in this direction, and the majority of the students did little more than, in the parlance of the day, "walk the hospital." The success that attended the efforts of these two teachers to organise systematically the methods of clinical instruction was a signal one, and crowds of students not only from other British schools, but also from the Continent and America, attended the Meath Hospital clinique. The principle in the new system of clinical teaching was diametrically opposed to that adopted by the "grinders," or "crammers" of the past as well as of the present day. It did not consist of "spoonfeeding" the students, and loading their minds with masses of facts available chiefly for purposes of examination, but consisted in a systematic effort "to teach the individual pupil, to encourage him to learn, to show him how to teach himself, to bring him into the true relation in which he ought to

[1] *British and Foreign Medical Review*, 1837, p. 287.

42

stand with his instructor, to make him familiar with bedside medicine, to show him the value of every new fact and observation in medicine, and to make him know the duty as well as make him taste the pleasure of original investigation."

The following extracts from his letters written at this time will show with what energy Stokes entered on his career as a public lecturer :—

"*April* 15, 1826.—On the night before my first lecture I sat up until past three in the morning transcribing what I had prepared. I did not finish the task, as, from sheer fatigue both of mind and body, I was obliged to relinquish it. At six in the morning, however, I sprang from bed and recommenced my labours, which I finished before breakfast. When the hour came crowds began to pour into the great theatre where I was to make my *début*. I found myself quite composed, though as I ascended the stairs an excellent fellow, who had all along shown the greatest anxiety about my success, said, 'Stokes, my dear fellow, you had better take a pinch of snuff, you look rather pale.' I felt all his kindness, but refused the offer. On entering the room I found it completely full, and the burst of applause which is intended always to encourage a young lecturer, agitated me

43

terribly. I, however, advanced to the table, and began with a tremulous voice, but after the first two or three sentences all my fear vanished ; I saw that I had rivetted the attention of my hearers, and feeling the importance of my subject I was carried away and every difficulty vanished. At the conclusion the applause was loud and long continued. All my friends came about me shaking hands and wishing me joy for my success. It was a proud moment, but soon followed by depression and violent headache. So after going round the wards I returned home."

In the autumn and winter of 1826 Dublin was visited by one of the severest epidemics of typhus that has occurred in Ireland during the present century. In the following extracts from letters written at the time by Stokes a graphic and ghastly picture is given of the appalling scenes that were of every-day occurrence during the epidemic :—

" *September* 17, 1826.—Were you in Dublin just now you would be shocked at the distress, aggravated by disease, under which the lower classes are labouring. They are literally lying in the streets under fever, turned by force out of their wretched lodgings, their bed the cold ground and the sky their only roof. We have now 240 cases [1] in the Meath Hospital of fever, and yet we are daily obliged to refuse admittance to crowds of miserable objects labouring under the severest form of the disease. God help the poor! I often wonder why any of them who can afford it should remain in this land of poverty and misrule. Government has now opened in different parts of the town hospitals with accommodation for 1,100 patients, and yet this is not half enough. I walked out the other night, and in passing by a lane my attention was arrested by a crowd or persons gathered in a circle round a group which occupied the steps of a hall door. This was a family consisting of a father, mother, and three wretched children who had been just expelled from their lodgings as having fever. The father was in high delirium, and as I approached him started off and ran down the street; the mother was lying at the foot of the door perfectly insensible, with an infant screaming on the breast, whence it had sought milk in vain; and the other two filled the air with their lamentations. It was a shocking sight indeed. No one would go near them to bring even a drop of cold water. In a short time, however, I succeeded in

[1] Shortly afterwards this hospital accommodated 300 fever patients.

having them all carried to the hospital, where they have since recovered."

"*October* 27, 1826.—I never remember Dublin in such a frightful state. As yet the fever raging here has not been very fatal, but the mortality is on the increase. It was at first one in forty, then it came down to one in thirty-five, and now it is one in twenty. It is calculated that should the epidemic go on in this way for a year one third of the inhabitants will have suffered fever. There are at present 1,414 beds in different hospitals open for fever patients, but this is a mere drop in the bucket. Were there five times the number open they would be filled in a day. I am working away preparing the winter's lectures; occupied from half-past seven in the morning till twelve at night just as hard as I can work at these, and with the hospital and my practice I am tolerably knocked up in the evening. My health is good, thank God, and my spirits are good also, except sometimes, when a cloud descends upon my mind and darkens all within. It is a great comfort that constant exposure to the infection diminishes the probability of taking this fever, and I now do not fear it in the slightest degree."

But his undaunted courage did not render him

46

proof against danger. In the following spring he received a poisoned wound in the hand while engaged in dissection and lay seriously ill for two days. The delicacy that ensued may have rendered him more susceptible of infection, and in March the fever seized him and nearly proved fatal. However, he battled through it, and in April we find him writing to the lady who was afterwards his wife from his father's country house in the Dublin hills where he had been sent to recruit.

"BALLINTEER, *April* 13, 1827.

"I am here at last, and systematically employed in recruiting my shattered health. I cannot express in words the delight I felt in once more breathing the free air of heaven and beholding the hills among which my childhood was passed clothed in all their splendid and varying hues. For eight months I have been immured in the smoky city, my mind constantly on the stretch—with hardly a moment I could call my own. This probation, ending in a long and painful illness, has given me a longing for rest and retirement of no usual intensity.

"The common earth, the air, the skies
To me are opening Paradise."

In April, 1828, Stokes was married to Miss Mary

Black, a lady four years his junior, to whom he had been attached since 1822, when he first met her at Milngavie, near Glasgow, and to whom he had been engaged for three years. She was the second daughter of Mr. John Black, of Glasgow, and his wife Margaret, daughter of Colonel MacNair. He brought his wife home to his father's house, No. 16, Harcourt Street, where they remained for upwards of three years.

## III

ASIATIC CHOLERA—CONTRIBUTIONS TO "LONDON
MEDICAL AND SURGICAL JOURNAL"—SWISS
TOUR—DEATH OF DR. MACNAMARA—CON-
TRIBUTIONS TO "CYCLOPÆDIA OF PRACTICAL
MEDICINE"

IN 1832 Asiatic cholera broke out in Ireland for
the first time in this country. In 1826 Graves
had lectured on this disease, and predicted its arrival
here. It reached Sunderland in 1831; but this pre-
diction, as he himself states, was not original with
him, for he had it from Dr. Brinkley,[1] who had also
foretold the failure of the potato crop and the conse-
quent famine in Ireland. It so happened that William
Stokes, together with the late Mr. Rumley, reported
the first case of the epidemic that appeared, and at no
small personal risk. They had been sent to inquire
into the cause of a sudden and mysterious death which
had occurred at Kingstown, then little more than a

[1] Lord Bishop of Cloyne.

seaside village. Neither of these physicians had ever seen a case of this disease, either before or after death. The result of their inspection, however, was that they pronounced the deceased to have died of the worst type of Asiatic cholera. Outside the house in which the body lay a crowd was anxiously awaiting their decision. The announcement was at first received with silent dismay, then came a burst of frenzy and indignation. A furious mob of men, women, and children hurled stones, mud, brickbats at them from all sides. They escaped injury almost by a miracle ; their carriage was battered and broken by the missiles thrown at them, and it was only by whip and spur that their postillion outstripped their pursuers. The outbreak of the disease in various parts of Ireland within a few days of this occurrence set all doubts as to its nature at rest and verified the conclusion that had been arrived at.

The lectures now contributed by William Stokes to the *London Medical and Surgical Journal* for two years proved the mainstay of this periodical. The first were a course of Clinical Lectures delivered at the Meath Hospital during the Sessions 1832–33. The second were delivered in the theatre of the Park Street School of Medicine, on the Theory and

Practice of Medicine. A writer in the *London Quarterly Journal* about this period classes him as a teacher with Crampton and Graves, and comments on his great success as a lecturer.

In 1832 he published clinical observations on the Exhibition of Opium,[1] and a paper on the Curability of Phthisis Pulmonalis.[2] In 1833 and 1834 he contributed various papers to the "London Cyclopædia of Practical Medicine," vols. ii. and iii. ; and in 1834 he became editor ot the *Dublin Journal of Medical Science*, in which periodical he brought out many valuable papers on Thoracic Pathology.[3]

In 1835 he commenced writing his work on the Diseases of the Chest, in which his object was to assist the researches of those already acquainted with the work of Laennec, Forbes, C. J. B. Williams, and James Clark, by guiding them into a path of accurate observation and of just reasoning upon physical signs and their association with symptoms, for, he says, " it is in this that the medical mind—the *mens medica*—is seen." Through the study of pathology he strove to remove the reproach of uncertainty under

[1] See *London Medical and Surgical Journal*, vol. i. ; *Dublin Journal of Medical Science*, 1st Series, p. 125 (1832).

[2] *London Medical and Surgical Journal*, vol. ii. p. 380.

[3] Vol. ii. p. 1, 1st Series ; vol. iii. p. 50 ; vol. xiv. p. 131.

which his art had hitherto laboured, and by the discovery and arrangement of facts to lift the diagnosis of disease into a science, placing it on a sure basis that time, with its mutations of opinion, can never shake.

In the summer of 1836 his health showed signs of breaking down. He was often disabled from work for days by headache, the acute pain in his temple "as a nail piercing to his brain," fits of depression came upon him, and his joyous, healthy nature was overshadowed by gloom. He was at last prevailed on to relax and take a month's holiday, and he writes afterwards, "My late depression was produced by my wretched health. I think that some dreadful malady would have attacked me had I not left home to travel."

The Rev. Sydney Smith, Mr. Grey, Mr. Perrin, and Mr. William MacDougall, were his companions on this tour. With the last mentioned he had contracted a strong friendship in boyhood, which lasted till death. Mr. MacDougall was a delightful companion. His passionate love of nature, high spirits, and daring love of adventure produced an effect like a wild sea breeze or bracing mountain air on the exhausted frame and over-worked brain of William

Stokes. Like boys set free from school they rushed along from town to town through Holland, Belgium, up the Rhine, and through the Alps, reaching home again in the short space of one month. The following extracts from his letters will help to show how deep was the impression then made, by the new scenes he visited, on his receptive and poetic nature.

" BRUSSELS, *August* 11, 1836.

" Friday week I left you, and here we are in the highest spirits, and, thank God, my head is behaving very well. We have seen Ostend, Bruges, Ghent, Antwerp. . . . At Bruges I had one of my splitting headaches, but it went off by noon. Here I first saw one of the wonderful cathedral churches of the Continent, with their glorious paintings and decorations. Everything was new, everything delightful. Each stone in the town seemed as if it were freshly polished. We strolled about from church to church until noon, when we dined and started by the canal for Ghent. We had a charming day, and as the gaily-painted and gilded barge glided silently along the canal, we lay on the quarter-deck covered with an awning and took our dessert of fruit with new delight. We passed through a wonderful country, flat as this sheet of paper, but cultivated, aye, every inch of it, in the highest degree. The fields are very small, and divided by sweet hedgerows, along which there grow a profusion of trees, so that, at a little distance, the effect of a forest was produced. The people here seemed happy as the day was long. Every five minutes we passed long boats laden with coal, often drawn by women ; but even these women were gay and happy. The coal barges were the cleanest things I ever saw. No soiling from the coal, which was in great blocks, all in their own places, and covered with painted boards, the ropes beautifully coiled up and perfectly white and clean. We wandered about Ghent, which is full of the most curious churches, and strolled through the dark, irregular lanes surrounding the cathedral and church of St. Jacob's and St. Michael's. At every step effects such as Prout so well represents were produced by the dark, massive towers of some old church or the wild, fantastic tracery of some Gothic arch, with its thousand ribs and ornaments worn and blackened by time. Over some of them eight centuries have passed, yet they are here still more beautiful than the day when the eye of their architect first rested on his completed labour. We started at an early hour ; as we entered the cathedral the service of the dead was being chaunted, and the organ pealed its wailing tone through our hearts. . . . Here we saw many great pictures by John of Bruges and Van Eyck, and a wonderful series of paintings of the life of Christ. Never did I see these subjects so handled before. In particular the angel comforting Christ, and the scourging. In the first the Saviour is seated leaning His head on the angel's breast looking up to him, with despair and hope so expressed and combined as to form a result altogether inconceivable. The scourging is an example of that true art of painting, on which you will see a chapter in the essays of Elia, an art by which the imagination is left to fill in the thing represented. The scourging is passed and the Redeemer lies bound and bleeding. He seems as if thrown at the foot of a mountain, alone, desecrated, and in torture. In the church of St. Michael there is Vandyke's Crucifixion, a beautiful painting, but it is a picture on which you look with more pleasure than pain. Everything is soft, rich, nay, voluptuous. Great as he was, he wanted his Master's strength and depth of feeling. He was taught to colour, but could not be taught to feel as a painter of the death of Christ should feel. Yesterday we tore ourselves from Ghent and travelled by diligence to Antwerp, passing through the richest part of the Low Countries, and we saw the great tower of the cathedral at a little before five o'clock. There it stood before us, six hundred feet high, with its open work sculpture and gossamer arches, tenants of the deep blue sky that stretched behind it. After reaching the hotel we rushed to the cathedral. The interior is different from anything I have yet seen. It is not overloaded with ornament, nor is the altar shut in by a screen, so that from the great door you look down to it through a long vista of plain, severe Gothic arches. It was getting dark, but we saw that most glorious of glorious pictures, the Descent from the Cross, by Rubens. After gazing on it my eyes dazzled and my heart palpitated, and I left it most unhappy, for I felt as though I knew nothing of it, and feared that I should not see it again."

" *August* 29.—The last three days have been perfectly delightful. Look at the map and trace us from Stuttgart to Ulm—on the glorious Danube—from thence to the Austrian extremity of the lovely lake of Constance, and then following the Rhine to its source among the Alps of the Grisons. Yesterday we spent visiting the extraordinary baths of Pfäfers. Imagine an Alpine valley richly wooded and running up for many miles through mountains of five, six, and seven thousand feet high. Their sides clothed with the most beautiful wood and green sward, and contrasting with the grander heights which were covered with eternal snow. Imagine the river of the gigantic valley roaring through a gorge three miles long and not more than from fifty to a hundred yards wide, and with perpendicular sides of 500 feet in height. At the bottom of this stands, on a natural table of stone, the bathhouse of the monks of the abbey, the most extraordinary place that can be well conceived. All supplies are let down by cords from the top of the mountain. We arrived here about noon, and sat down at the *table d'hôte*, at which the Abbot presided. We were surrounded by bilious Germans, rheumatic Russians, and green-sick girls from the Tyrol. They all looked wretchedly ill, and no wonder, for they have to live in a house where the sun hardly shines, and to drink warm water and sour beer. After dinner we went to see the source of the hot spring, but this is a scene which cannot be described. It is too extraordinary, too sublime for me to convey any idea of it to you. To-day we passed through the Via Mala, a road cut through the living rock along a gorge of fifteen hundred feet in depth, and so narrow that in many places we could throw a stone against the opposite side. But I cannot describe it to you with its roaring river a thousand feet beneath us, and its lightning-blasted pines, and its beauties and horrors. The great difficulty in this country is to adapt yourself to its giant magnitude. A mountain seems within a mile of you when it is six or eight miles off. You think it about eight hundred feet high. It is three or four thousand, and so on."

In connection with the visit to Pfäfers, once so celebrated and fashionable a resort, Stokes used to relate an amusing anecdote. During a conversation he had with one of the local physicians, who was dilating with enthusiasm on the magically curative effects of the waters on all sorts and conditions of disease, Stokes asked, for his own information, something about the composition of these far-famed waters. The answer, if not scientific, was certainly friendly : "Well ! as you are a bro-ther, I will tell you : they do contain no-thing ! "

On his return home Stokes resumed his large practice, commenced lectures at the hospital, and could seize only occasional intervals for working at his book on the Chest. He writes : "I am now quite well ;

I am not working too hard at the desk. Indeed, I have no time to do so, for I am kept very full of practice." In October he went to visit Dr. Macnamara, who had fallen ill while visiting in the county of Mayo, and whom he brought back to Dublin.

" *October* 27, 1836.—You will be sorry to hear that I have been for two days down to Connemara, to see poor Macnamara. He is dying. Oh ! what a tragedy it will be ! We expect him up to town this week. I never saw the glorious Lough Corrib look so beautiful. I was entertained by Miss Blake ; she is a perfect specimen of the old Irish aristocracy. Tall, distinguished, elegantly formed, with dark hair and exquisitely fair complexion ; she looked, as she stood in her tapestried hall, a lady of romance ; her youth, her mourning dress, her classic head, and the symbols of her loved religion, all combined to form a picture not easily to be forgotten. The castle, grey and worn, stands on a green platform over the clear and rapid river through which the whole waters of Lough Mask and Lough Corrib rush to the sea. It reverses Byron's simile, 'All green and wildly fresh without,' &c., &c. You will say I am raving ; but in truth a little time will level these ancient castles, and their highborn and honourable inhabitants, and the feelings which their communion creates, and then 'utility' will have its reign, and 'common sense,' laughing at the past and the beautiful, will build factories with the remains of history, make money, and die."

"*November* 25, 1836.—I should have answered your letter before but that I really had no time, not as much as would have sufficed to write even a note ; and this letter I write from the drawing-room of poor Macnamara, who is rapidly approaching his deliverance from this world's cares, and sorrows and sufferings. He has just asked me, 'Stokes, am I dying?' I told him the truth. His answer was, 'Don't leave me.' So I am staying here to watch him to the last. He is scarcely suffering, and, indeed, the act of death is almost always painless. It is a natural change without unnecessary suffering ; and are not these delusions of hope, these plans for hereafter, that incredulity as to approaching death, are not these provisions, merciful provisions, to smooth the dark way from earth to immortality ? Even when the departing being seems in agony he is often not so. The limbs may be convulsed and the respiration laboured, yet without pain or consciousness even of the apparent suffering. We pass away silently, calmly. The struggle is seen but not felt."

Early in the following year his wife was in Scotland watching by her mother's death-bed. Mrs. Black was a fine example of the high-bred Scottish lady of the old school. She died in March, 1837, and Stokes writes to his wife : " This is not the first time that we have tasted the bitterness of death, nor will it be the last, but seek to be tranquil, for you have high duties to perform here ; be a consolation to your dear sisters who are the greatest sufferers now, and may God's peace be around you. You must bear up for your children's sake, and not yield too much. I had hoped up to this evening to be able to go over, but fate seems to forbid it. I worked last night till half-past eleven in hopes of being able to start by the *Mercury* this morning, but it was not to be ; then I trusted to be able to go to-night, but now three of my patients are dangerously ill, and I cannot, ought not, to leave them. . . . May God preserve you in your hour of sorrow.

" I have resolved on taking the house (Mount Malpas) at Killiney ; it will be such a peaceful and beautiful retreat for you and your dear, dear sisters, and I shall have finished my book now in three days. . . ."

The book alluded to here was the above-mentioned work on the chest.

During the years 1833–35 his labours, both medical
and literary, were unremitting. He did not confine
himself to the subjects on which he is best known as
an authority, for in the " Cyclopædia of Practical
Medicine," to which he was at this time a frequent
contributor, are to be found articles by him on
dysphagia, enteritis, gastritis, gastro-enteritis, inflammation of the liver, and peritonitis.

Of these papers probably the most important is that
on " Peritonitis from Perforation of the Serous Membrane." He credits Graves with having revolutionised
the practice hitherto adopted in the treatment of this
disease by the bold administration of opium in place
of the routine treatment then in use of bleeding and
purgatives. The system advocated by Stokes was "to
support the strength of the patient so as to gain time
and to diminish as far as possible the peristaltic action
of the intestine."

In connection with this subject the author of an
able article on the life and work of Stokes,[1] observes
of Stokes and Graves that, guided by these principles,
these eminent men discarded bleeding and purgatives
and boldly administered opium in such quantities and
with such striking benefit to the patient as to change

[1] See *Birmingham Medical Review*, April, 1878.

the whole aspect of the therapeutics of this disorder. The ordinary physician is now well acquainted with all this. At the time, however, when these researches were published, the treatment of peritonitis was little more than a "contemplation of death." We believe that no single improvement in the medical art, except the use of anæsthetics, can be placed on a level with the one now described. A host of important therapeutic applications necessarily occurred as direct inferences from the principles and practice here laid down. We in these days find it difficult to think of the treatment of peritonitis, whether arising from internal causes or from the operations of the surgeon, as apart from the use of opium, but this great advance we owe to the insight and clinical skill of Graves and Stokes. Alike in foreign countries and at home they have obtained due credit for their work in this particular, for a solid step in advance had been achieved by them. Had they done nothing else, mankind would have good cause to hold them in remembrance.

## IV

## Work on Diseases of the Chest

A S the result of several years of increasing labour
in private practice, in clinical teaching in the
Meath Hospital, and in lecturing in the Park Street
School of Medicine, the work of Stokes on the Diagnosis and Treatment of Diseases of the Chest appeared
in the year 1837. Sir Dominic (then Dr.) Corrigan,
in his exhaustive review of this book, says that its
appearance was "hailed with delight both by those
who love their profession as a science, and by those
who more humbly but not less usefully cultivate it
as a practical art, seeking in each new page that is
presented to them the means of curing or alleviating
disease." [1]

Prior to the works of Corvisart and Laennec little
or nothing had been done in elucidating the phenomena
of thoracic disease. Laennec's work first appeared in

[1] *Dublin Medical Journal*, vol. xi. p. 466.

1819, a second edition having been published in 1826, and to this celebrated author must be given the credit of the discovery, explanation, and connection of physical signs with organic changes, and with the symptoms and history of the case, the importance of testing the value of physical *signs* by the history and *symptoms* of the disease, which in their turn should be corrected by the physical signs. Stokes carried on this line of investigation, it being his belief that progress in any art is gradual and cautious, that the wisest worker rises on the shoulders of his predecessor. Men should, as it were, "enter in" to the labour of other men, and to advance knowledge one should be content to take up the thread where the last investigator laid it down, and from that point to carry on his work. Speaking of Laennec's "imperishable volume," Corrigan observed that "it would have seemed almost unpardonable heresy to have criticised or added to it, and accordingly, until the appearance of the present work, we have had little more than compilations in various shapes and forms of the original. It required power and talent of no ordinary range to add to the production, to supply the omissions, and to correct the errors of such a master." These effects Sir Dominic believed were achieved in Stokes' work.

After the publication of Laennec's work, Stokes observed that the followers of Laennec, as a natural result of his discoveries, neglected to attend to the fact that " physical signs only reveal mechanical conditions which may proceed from the most different causes, and that the latter are to be determined by a process of reasoning on their connection and succession, on their relation to time, *and their association with symptoms.*" The result of this mistake often was that the diagnosis founded on physical signs did not coincide with that obtained from symptoms, a circumstance which at the time gave unmixed satisfaction to the opponents of Laennec and his discovery. A good result, however, followed this mistake, for it fixed on the mind of the physician more firmly than it would otherwise have done the necessity for " the close connection of the study of physical signs with that of symptoms, so as to illustrate their mutual bearing on diagnosis, and remove that unjust opprobrium thrown on the advocates of auscultation that they neglect the study of symptoms " [1]

It should always be remembered that physical signs of themselves are frequently of permanent importance, and Stokes' remarks on this point, Sir D. Corrigan observes, should never be forgotten.

[1] " A Treatise on the Diagnosis and Treatment of Diseases of the Chest." Preface. 1837.

" It is in the curable diseases that their great value is seen. Indeed, in a large proportion of such cases, *the first effect of treatment is to render disease latent, and to cause an absolute necessity for the study of physical signs.*"

The work commences by an exposition of the peculiarities of the anatomy and physiology of the thorax, peculiarities which render it more adapted for the production of physical signs than either the cranial or abdominal cavities.

" If we take a general view of the cranial, thoracic, and abdominal cavities, it would appear that in none of them is the diagnosis of disease from symptoms so difficult as in the chest. But further investigation will prove to us that there is no cavity in the disease of which, when we combine the study of symptoms properly so called with that of physical signs, the determination of the nature, extent, and modification of disease is so easy and certain."

Of the nine sections into which Stokes divides his book the second—that on bronchitis—is the most voluminous and exhaustive. In fact, it includes the consideration of topics which are remote from the inflammatory affection of the bronchi, such as dilatation and atrophy of their terminations themselves.

As one of the reviewers of the work has said, "It appears to be a prominent aim of the author to make the study of bronchitis a key to thoracic pathology."

This work offers many examples of the author's exceptional power of description. It is, as Dr. Sibson has said, a "series of living pictures of disease;" and Dr. Hudson has observed, "It is the pictorial power which gives such vividness and reality to Dr. Stokes' delineations of disease, combining close reasoning with artistic power and comprehensive grasp of his subject." Thus when speaking of the appearance and symptoms of patients labouring under what he states may be termed congestive bronchitis, those accustomed to see the disease will at once recognise the passage as a picture from nature, "The physiognomy is most characteristic, the complexion is generally of a dusky hue, and the countenance, though with an anxious and melancholy expression, has in several cases a degree of fulness which contrasts remarkably with the condition of the rest of the body. . . . The nostrils are dilated, thickened, and vascular. The lower lip is enlarged, and its mucous membrane everted and livid, giving a peculiar expression of anxiety, melancholy, and disease to the countenance. The shoulders are elevated and brought forward, and the patient stoops habitually, a habit contracted in his various fits of orthopnœa and cough, and the relief which is experienced from inclining the body forwards. Thus even in bed we often find these patients sitting up, with their arms folded, and resting on their knees, and the head bent forwards, the object of which seems to be to relax the abdominal muscles and to substitute the mechanical support of the arms for that of muscles, which would interfere with inspiration." [1]

It would not, in the writer's opinion, be in accordance with the object or design of this work if he were to discuss in detail, or attempt an exhaustive analysis of Stokes' "Treatise on Diseases of the Chest"; this has already been done on more than one occasion, and a repetition of such efforts appears therefore unnecessary and uncalled for. The most important results, however, of the researches embodied in the treatise may be indicated :—

1. The discovery of a stage of pneumonia prior to that described by Laennec as the first.

---

[1] "A Treatise on the Diagnosis and Treatment of Diseases of the Chest," by William Stokes, p. 177.

2. The observation that contraction of the side has sometimes followed the cure of pneumonia.

3. The recognition of a fibrous layer in the pulmonary pleura.

4. That paralysis of the intercostal muscles and diaphragm may result from pleuritic inflammation, causing a yielding or bulging of these muscles when exposed to the pressure of liquid effusion.

5. The discovery of a new displacement of the heart in consequence of the rapid absorption of pleuritic effusion in the right side.

6. That paralysis of the muscular tissues of the bronchial tubes is an etiological factor in the production of their dilatation.

7. The application of auscultation to the study of croup and the classification or division of that disease into primary and secondary.

8. The employment of the stethoscope as an aid to the detection of foreign bodies in the air passages.

9. The invention of a graduated spring calipers for the accurate measurements of the contractions or dilatations of the chest, and determining its changes from time to time under the influence of disease.

In Ireland the appearance of this work was warmly

welcomed by the profession, among whom he numbered many true and honoured friends. It placed
the author at once in the front rank of the profession in Dublin, as it was felt that no work that
had previously emanated, from the Irish School of
Medicine had done more to raise it in the estimation of the world. In England it was received as
the one work of the time which justified students
of Medicine in the hope that their art was at length
"really beginning to assume the character of an
inductive science, and in Germany it was declared
unequalled since the time of Laennec." [1]

Of this work Sir Henry Acland, Regius Professor
of Medicine in the University of Oxford, has written
in a still more eulogistic manner. He observed that
"the terseness of his language and clearness of his
statements produced a profound impression on
vigorous and active minds at the time. The precise
summaries at the end of the various chapters, notably
that of the physical signs of diseases of the pleura,

[1] In the preface of the translation into German of the work the trans-
lator, Dr. Gerhard Von dem Busch (" Abhandlung über die Diagnose und
Behandlung der Brust-Krankheiten aus dem Englischen von Gerhard
von dem Busch." Bremen, 1838) observed, " Since the publication of
Laennec's great work, which formed an epoch in medical history, many
valuable treatises have appeared in France and England on the same
subject, but none of them can bear comparison with that which has
lately emanated from the pen of Dr. William Stokes."

seemed almost a revelation both in statement of fact and drawing of inference."

Shortly after its publication honorary distinctions were literally showered on Stokes both at home and abroad. The degree of M.D. was conferred on him —*honoris causâ*—by the University of Dublin; he was elected a Fellow of the King and Queen's College of Physicians in Ireland, and an honorary member of the Imperial Academy of Medicine, Vienna, and of the Royal Medical Societies of, Berlin, Leipsic, Edinburgh, and Ghent; of the Medical Societies of the Grand Duchy of Baden, the Medico-Chirurgical Society of Hamburg, and the National Institute of Philadelphia.

## V

FRIENDSHIPS—LOVE FOR MUSIC AND THE DRAMA
—SHAKESPEARE READINGS—AIMS AND OBJECTS
OF ART—PROFESSOR MAHAFFY—THOMAS CAR-
LYLE—FOREIGN TOURS

IN the years of increased labour which followed
the publication of this work on the chest, it is
easy to conceive how much refreshment and support
Stokes gained by intercourse with friends whose labours
lay outside his own field. On the other hand, we
have already seen an instance of how his sympathy in
their pursuits acted as a stimulus to them, while the
following letter written to Petrie when he was collect-
ing material for his work on the Round Towers of
Ireland, will show this sympathy developing into
practical aid. It may be well to explain that on the
eve of his departure for a holiday on the Continent
after the publication of his book, Petrie had confided
to him his belief that the continental church towers

of the Carlovingian age were of the same type as those of Ireland, this idea having first occurred to him on seeing the representation of a cylindrical tower with conical top on the ancient seal of Aix-la-Chapelle.

"To George Petrie, LL.D.

"Andermatt on the St. Gothard Pass,

"*Friday, August* 16, 1839.

"My dearest Friend,—Here I am with my little party storm-bound on the summit of this sublime pass ! If you will look at a map of Germany and Switzerland you can trace our route through the Low Countries to Cologne on the Rhine, up the river to Manheim, then by Heidelberg, Baden, the Black Forest, Schaffhausen, Zurich, Lucerne, and St. Gothard. Through all my wanderings I have ever thought how you would enjoy these glorious scenes, but you would make a slow traveller, for I think it would be impossible to get you away from some of the places that we have visited, or driven past. I have pictured you and your dear family in my mind's eye, luxuriating in the view of Cologne Cathedral or Antwerp, or boating on the face of the Lake of Lucerne. I hope the time will come when we may go over this ground together. . . .

I have not forgotten the Round Towers. I examined the Church of Aix-la-Chapelle with a good deal of care, and also looked for such representations of it as I could find in the old paintings in the Church. Most of the paintings, however, are frescoes of a date much later than the building as it stands at present; even later than the choir which was added to the more ancient polygonal structure. I did not, however, see the old shrines and reliquaries, and it is on these that the most reliable representation of the original church may be looked for. At Cologne, however, I took great pains in examining the reliquaries. Here there are two very magnificent shrines, one of the three kings and the other of St. Engelbert. They are of gold and silver, set with precious stones and covered with chasing and exquisite filigree work. On the shrine of the three kings there are numerous representations of saints holding in their hands the churches they have founded and dedicated, but I think they are representations of basilicas apparently massive, irregular, low buildings covering a considerable extent of ground, and many of them presenting a circular apartment covered by a low dome supported on a low polygonal tower. The arches are round-headed. In none of these reliefs

could I discover a 'Round Tower.' On the shrine
of St. Engelbert, however, I found one, and only one.
It stands at one of the angles of a great square tower.
The representation is modelled in high relief, and to
my eye it seems like a most perfect likeness of one of
the Irish Round Towers. It enlarges slightly towards
the base and is quite circular. It has the low conical
roof and the windows towards the summit with one
window at the usual distance from the base. I asked
my sister-in-law to take a little sketch of this tower of
which I send you a rough copy.

"Now, as to my next observation. In the Church
of St. Thomas at Strasburg, I was startled to see two
towers so like the Irish towers that they brought back
many of our rambles to my memory. The Church is
evidently an old one. It is quite in the Lombard
style, and I should say the older Lombardic. The
eastern apse is polygonal, rising to a vast height, surrounded by a gallery with a double row of arches;
the lower are of great size and not open. The upper
small and open. The two round towers each face a
side of the square tower-like apse. They are very
similar *externally*, but one is about twice as high as
the other. There are no similar towers near the
church, so that their position with regard to the apse,

produces an irregular and singular effect. The lowest of these towers is evidently the most ancient and my reasons for this opinion are as follows :—

" 1. The higher tower contains a spiral staircase of stone, which leads to the gallery, and it seems more in harmony with the rest of the building both from its height and position, the apex corresponding to the keystone of the arch, which it nearly touches. This tower is of brick.

" 2. The lower tower just reaches above the lower gallery of the apse. Its diameter is less than that of the high tower, and a segment of the tower has been cut off to make way for the gallery. Looking through one of the little windows at this point, I could see dimly into the interior of the tower. It has no staircase, and its foundation is lost in the buildings below. The sacristan told me that there was no entrance into it from below, that it had been built up altogether. I descended into the vaults, but could find nothing. I I believe the high tower was built in imitation of the old one. This church should be most accurately examined. . . ."

The twelve years following the appearance of his work on diseases of the chest were those of deepest interest. It has been more than once observed by William Stokes, that during the first quarter of the present century, the mind of Ireland was sunk in apathy and dejection, and there was a marked decline of intellectual vitality. But in the period from 1830 to 1850 a singular development of intellect and energy in almost every department of mental culture showed itself. In art and literature, Petrie and Frederic William Burton, Samuel Ferguson, Thomas Davis, Clarence Mangan,[1] and Anster were doing good work, while in science the labours of our leading men were crowned by discovery. " Hamilton furnished the most

[1] The following account of the tragical death of Clarence Mangan, from the pen of the distinguished authoress, Miss Jane Barlow, in a letter to Miss Guiney, who has recently brought out an edition of Mangan's poems, will be read with interest. She mentions with regard to Dr. Stokes that he was in fact Mangan's last friend. For Mangan had been lost sight of by everybody for a very long time, when one morning, as Stokes was going his rounds in the Meath Hospital, the porter told him that admission was asked for a miserable-looking man at the door. He was shocked to find that this was Mangan, who said to him, " You are the first who has spoken one kind word to me for many years "—a terrible saying. Stokes got him a private room, and had everything possible done for him ; but not many days after he died. Immediately after death, such a wonderful change came over the face that Stokes hurried away to Sir Frederic Burton, the artist, and said to him, " Clarence Mangan is lying dead at the hospital. I want you to come and look at him, for you never saw anything so beautiful in your life ! " So Sir Frederic came, and made the sketch which is now in the National Gallery. And so, " suddenly and quietly as the shutting of a glow-worm's little lamp," on the 20th of June, 1849, his life went out. Only three persons are said to have followed his body to the grave.

advanced instrument of investigation, the Calculus of Quaternions, leading to paths hitherto unexplored," while the papers of McCullagh on geometry, and on physical optics, "are distinguished," says William Stokes, "by his power of giving to his researches that peculiar symmetry in their results, which is such an element of the beautiful in science."

The tie that bound William Stokes to these men was something more than ordinary friendship. Unversed as he was in the practical part, the technical work of the artist, and ignorant of higher mathematics, it was yet wonderful what sympathy and support these men derived from him, with what ardour his genius could reverberate to theirs. In the genial atmosphere he created around him, they seemed to live their fullest life, and those of them who died before him died beneath his care.

The love of poetry and art seemed to be innate with him. As a child his chief delight, as already stated, was in reading ballads from the Border Minstrelsy of Sir Walter Scott, as he often did when sitting on the top of a wall, near his sisters while they sketched. They had been carefully trained by O'Conor and George Petrie, and were landscape painters of no mean skill. The pleasure that their brother William found in watching Nature in all her moods was no doubt fostered in him by the example of these sisters, who were some years older than he, and both of whom were distinguished by untiring industry and conscientiousness, as well as by the exquisite delicacy of their work. At the period of which we speak, George Petrie and Frederic Burton were the painters in whose works William Stokes, as a lover both of Nature and of his country, took most delight. Each of them, in his own way, and according to his power, were striving to do with the pencil for Ireland that which Scott had done for his country with the pen— to paint her scenery and native character as seen through the medium of a keen and appreciative eye. At this period Petrie had given us such works as Ardfinnen Castle, The Twelve Pins of Connemara, The Black Valley, and The Pilgrims at Clonmacnois; and Frederic Burton was at work on The Blind Girl at the Holy Well, The Arran Fisherman's Drowned Child, and The Connemara Toilet, &c.

To William Stokes, their works were the embodiments of a poetry and charm in the native character of Ireland, which he had felt and loved through life. The wild freshness and grace, the deep pathetic tenderness which lies in Irish music, were here translated into dramatic paintings by the one ; while the other, when faithfully representing the ancient monuments of Ireland, strove "to connect with them the expression of human feelings equally belonging to our history." The landscape painting of Petrie was described by William Stokes as bearing a striking resemblance to the poetry of Wordsworth. "In both the painter and the poet," he says, "we find the same perception of the beautiful, the same dwelling on scenes of simple nature, the same use of natural objects as means to an end, that end being the elevation of the heart, and the training of the mind to thoughts of purity and love."

One influence was added which more perhaps than any other at this time helped to develop in him that love for poetry, and especially dramatic poetry, which had been a passion with him from boyhood. It was now that Helen Faucit[1] came to Ireland, bearing with her letters of introduction from Sir Archibald Alison, the brother of Professor Alison, of Edinburgh, Stokes' teacher and warm friend. She at once found herself, as it were, in her natural atmosphere when

[1] Now Lady Martin, authoress of "Some of Shakespeare's Female Characters." William Blackwood and Sons, 1885.

she entered the home-like circle that had risen round the hearth at Merrion Square, while all her genius warmed and expanded among those who grew to love her there. William Stokes at once recognised in her the true painter of that human nature, of which he had so profound a knowledge, and he saw in her impersonations the noblest realisation of woman as he had always conceived her—"Woman the depository of all that is pure, and delicate, and moral in this life." That his respect was fully esteemed by her who was its object, may be seen by the following letter written after his death :—

"BRYNTISILIO, LLANGOLLEN, 1880.

"I wish I could express in words what I owed to your dear father. When first I knew him, I was young in my art and in years—knew little of life and that little often sad and discouraging—entirely distrustful of myself, often wondering how I found the courage, when all was so weary, as to persevere. He first felt with me, seemed to guess how my heart asked for sympathy, and without my telling of a trouble, he gave me bounteously the sweet rain of encouragement, for want of which my heart felt dried up and withering.

82

" His taste was so fine, his judgment so deep, his sympathy so large, and yet so fond and tender in all things. Such a character was a revelation to me.

" I seemed to have been fumbling in the dark before. I knew well what I wanted, but did not know how to reach it. He revealed to me myself— at least, he discovered what I was feeling and wanting to bring forth in my art. He showed it to me, and by a word I felt that as it were revealed. I had had a light thrown in my way—a torch to encourage and guide me upward.

" He gave me credit for such good inspirations that I felt my courage grow and expand towards them. Shall I ever forget seeing him and your dear mother and their children in the same place, night after night, of ' Antigone ' and, indeed, of almost all my characters. He thought I had intuitions about things, natural instincts. Do you remember, in the madness of Belvidera and Isabella, the difference which he noticed that I made in each—how right he said it was, mentally and physically, the suddenness of the one, the slow going and coming of the reason in the other— how it tottered before it gave way. How I wish now I could have given him my notion of Ophelia's madness. But, then, there never was an actor that he could have borne in 'Hamlet'!

"How keen his sensibility was! It seemed to hurt him to see a Shakesperian part wrongly felt. I never asked his advice. He was so modest he would have said he knew nothing about it, and yet, by the way, I could turn the talk, and by a casual word I could fish up what I wanted from him."

We have shown what an ardent lover of Shakespeare Stokes had been all through his life, and in his later years he took great interest in Shakespeare readings inaugurated by the Rev. Robert Perceval Graves, of Dublin, the meetings being held in turn at the respective houses of the members of a little Shakespeare Society. Among the readers may be mentioned Dr. Ingram, Professor Mahaffy, Sir Samuel and Lady Ferguson, Professor Dowden, Dr. Salmon, Lord O'Hagan, and others. It was most interesting to note the different way in which these readers (all men possessed of much literary ability, and actuated by the deepest reverence of the poet) interpreted his thoughts and discussed his meanings, while some of the readers, such as Stokes himself, when he took such a part as that of Caliban in the "Tempest," showed no little dramatic power.

In connection with the aims and objects of art the following remarks, taken from a letter of William Stokes, will be read with interest :—

"It has been said that the real end and object of art is to deliver in its varied language the light-imparting message of God to man, and for this purpose to avail itself of every human feeling, sympathy, and perfection, physical as well as moral. And it is plain that whosoever establishes a single new means to so great an end and adds it to the bright apparatus of the past, the painter, the sculptor, the architect, actor, and musician, must claim a high place in the world's esteem.

"In the pursuit of art, we would avoid getting into that condition which has been suitably termed 'mental luxury'; one which generates selfishness, on the one hand, and indolence on the other—a condition in which we become recipients, but not artificers, and in the dreamy, idle contemplation of the beautiful become the slaves of a refined sensualism. There is too much of this tendency at the present time ; and the facility with which great works of art can be seen and studied, or exquisite engravings, possessing much of the beauty of the originals be obtained, assist in this indulgence in the sentimentalism of art a feeling most unwholesome and hostile to true progress. We are not to worship art, but to use it as a means to some great end. All things speak of God ; His revelations are infinite, but our means of receiving them are not unlimited. We are given intellect, feeling, sympathy, and sense, as the avenues by which we may receive the truth, and there is no man in which some of these channels may not be opened so as to imbibe that he may afterwards emit the light. The intellect is addressed by reason supported by education. But art teaches by other methods—in unwritten tongues, in varied languages ; it preaches truth through beauty, and tells of the God of love, of beauty, strength, and power. It does not teach by dogma, nor by an array of evidence ; nor does it convince by terror, nor is its indirect influence less important when it acts less by teaching than by inducing us to learn ; by shedding around and within us the pure effluences of beauty and of truth, so that the darkness and the hardness of our nature and the evils of our position, for the hour at least, disappear. Our load of evil is lightened and our minds and natures more easily pursue a heavenward path—

# FRIENDSHIPS, TASTES, HOME LIFE

> "'As plants in mines that never saw the sun,
> But upward climb, and strive to get to him.'"

"When I first came to know William Stokes in 1858," writes Professor Mahaffy,[1] one of William Stokes' most esteemed friends, "his house had been for years the resort of all the wit and all the learning which Ireland possessed. His fame brought all foreign visitors of literary note with introductions to see him. He kept open house, and in addition to his large family, some learned foreigner or some stray country wit could be met with almost daily at his simple but most hospitable table."

His house gradually formed a nucleus for the intellectual and musical society of Dublin ; and foreigners, whether professional men or artists, were made especially welcome. On Christmas Day especially he desired that foreigners should be invited to join his circle at dinner who would otherwise have felt their exile from home at this especial season. On one such occasion several different nationalities were represented at his board.

The Saturday evenings were generally given to music and conversation, and on gala nights, and at

---

[1] "Dr. William Stokes ; A Personal Sketch," by Rev. J. P. Mahaffy, D.D., *Macmillan's Magazine*, February, 1878.

his children's festivals, he would preside at puppet-shows, and act charades and throw himself heart and soul into this as into any other pursuit in life.

" This period," writes his sister, "was perhaps his happiest ; he had youth, enthusiasm, love, children, and was surrounded by troops of warm and sympathetic friends, among whom were Dr. Gregory, of Edinburgh ; Major Patrickson and Barton, old Peninsular officers ; George Petrie and Col. Pratt, artists ; William Archer Butler, Drs. Porter and Barker, Graves, Apjohn, Wilde, Cæsar, and J. Hastings Otway, and many others."

Had it not been for the good effects of such social life and the complete rest and relaxation that he thus obtained, he never could have borne the fatigue of his enormous work for so many years. But the benefit of such influences was not merely personal. The revival from the condition of intellectual torpor that had prevailed in society in Dublin for a quarter of a century was materially aided by these brilliant and easy reunions, where an imaginative genius and his wife's kindly grace shed their influences over all assembled at his house.

Professor Mahaffy has said of the young friends whom Stokes loved to see about him, that " many of them date their first inspiration for work and disgust for idleness to the influence of his refined and literary home. There are those, too, who have confessed that his spirit turned them from the vices and follies of youth, and led them to a serious and honourable view of their duties amid the temptations of a college career. And yet he never preached sermons, or gave any formal moral advice. He was far too subtle and original a teacher to follow so well-beaten and idle a track. Nor was this stimulating influence confined to the young. On the topics which he touched he made all those around him rise above themselves and do greater and better work. Thus the remarkable researches of George Petrie, both on the antiquities and music of Ireland, would never have seen the light but for the constant pressure and encouragement of William Stokes, who, though he was neither a musician nor an artist, felt the beauty of artistic work with a keenness and a tenderness beyond the depth of ordinary men. In this way he was a great schoolmaster to all those about him—a man who might have been a great scholastic head, just as his powers of observation might have made him one of the first naturalists of the time." [1]

[1] *Macmillan's Magazine*, p. 301, February, 1878.

In this year (1849) Thomas Carlyle visited Ireland and brought an introduction to Stokes who hospitably received him, and invited several literary friends, including Drs. Todd, Petrie, Frederic Burton, and others, to meet him at dinner. The impression that Carlyle made on Stokes was the reverse of favourable. His self-assertiveness, intolerance of any opposition to his views, vanity, and unconcealed contempt for everything and every one in the country in which he was an honoured guest, struck Stokes as being as ill-mannered as it was low-bred. He used to say that he had during his life-time met many men who were in every sense of the word *bores*, but that " Carlyle was hyperborean " ! It is not surprising therefore, that Stokes, whom Carlyle described as being a " rather fierce, sinister looking man," became as the evening wore on, " more and more gloomy, emphatic, and contradictory," and we can well believe that after 11 o'clock p.m. Carlyle was " glad to get away."[1]

As a conversationalist Stokes was matchless, though perhaps, in the presence of any one who was prim and matter-of-fact, he took somewhat too keen a pleasure in astonishing and mystifying him by some extravagant

[1] " Reminiscences of my Irish Journey in 1849," by Thomas Carlyle, 1882, p. 50.

paradox, which he would support by the most subtle and ingenious arguments. As a storyteller also he was unrivalled ; the pungency of his wit, his innate poetic instinct, and deep feeling, all combining to render his descriptions, whether of tragic or comic incidents in his own life or that of others, examples of word-painting such as are seldom met with. As an illustration of his readiness and wit, it may be mentioned that on one occasion he was called on to give evidence in a case involving the interests of one of his patients. There had previously been many complaints made as to the insanitary condition of the court, especially in reference to alleged defective ventilation. After Stokes had given his evidence, the judge, with very questionable taste observed : " Dr. Stokes, before you leave the court, I should be greatly obliged if you would give an opinion as to whether you think the ventilation of this court is likely to prove injurious to the health of those who are compelled to remain here for many hours every day ? " " I think, my lord," replied Stokes, " that the best way to answer your question would be to suggest this motto for your court, ' Fiat Justicia ruat cælum ! ' " But whatever topic ¡ was the subject of conversation either in his home circle or elsewhere, one thing he did instinctively, he strove to raise its tone to a high level, and without appearing to aim at this, he made others about him endeavour to do likewise. This was one of the secrets of his success as a great clinical teacher, and one which so often had the happy result of kindling the sacred fire of enthusiasm, "the genius of sincerity" in his pupils.

Among his home recreations, there was none that afforded him keener delight than music, in which several members of his family possessed both aptitude and technical skill. He was not himself a musician, but had an instinctive power of knowing and appreciating what was good in music. What appeared to afford him the greatest pleasure were the simple national melodies of his own and other countries. His taste for the former was largely fostered by his lifelong friend George Petrie, who, in addition to many other artistic accomplishments, possessed a sound theoretical as well as practical knowledge of music. Petrie was an industrious collector of Irish national melodies, many of which have been skilfully arranged both by the late Frank Hoffmann and Professor Villiers Stanford. But William Stokes' musical taste was not confined to the national music of his own country. That of other countries gave him almost as great a pleasure, particularly, I should say, that of Italy and Hungary. The writer has a vivid recollection of a musical experience he had many years ago, when travelling in the Austrian Tyrol with his father. They halted one evening at a village not far from Ischl, and after dinner a band of Bohemian Gypsies commenced to play their national melodies outside the inn. Stokes' delight knew no bounds. He rushed out, sat down among the musicians, gave a liberal order for refreshments for the band, with the happy result that the concert was protracted far into the night !

But his taste was not confined to this simple, and what might be termed elementary music, for though he never would have appreciated the modern German School of Wagner and his followers, the works of Handel, Mozart, Weber, and Gluck, as well as those of many composers of the early Italian school, such as Pergolese, Stradella, Marcello, &c., were sources of never failing delight to him.

With such tastes, such exceptional powers of accurate observation, such a love for what is beautiful in Nature and in Art, such a power of seeing, even in objects that to most people would be insignificant, something worthy of observation and note, it can be

readily understood what a delightful and interesting
travelling companion he was. The writer had exceptional opportunities of observing these rare and exceptional qualities, having on several occasions been his
companion in tours through the Western Highlands of
Ireland and Scotland, in Germany, Austria, Bavaria,
France, and Spain, and of these Spain appeared to
afford him the greatest pleasure and interest. Its
romantic literature, and eventful history ; its splendid
cathedrals, palaces, and fortresses ; the art productions
of Velasquez, Murillo, and Ribera ; the examples of
the severest as well as the most florid types of Gothic
architecture; the picturesque costumes of the peasantry
and their simple and primitive modes of life ; the
remains of the Roman, Gothic, and Moorish occupa-
tions of the country—all combined·to give him the
keenest pleasure, and furnish him in his latter days
with some of the happiest reminiscences of his life.
In places remote from art collections, his practical
knowledge of geology, mineralogy, and botany,
enabled him always to find objects of interest, which
the unobservant traveller would undoubtedly pass by,
unnoticed and uncared for.

But it must not be supposed that he did not take
an equal, perhaps in some respects a greater, delight

in the scenery and historic structures, ecclesiastical as well as military, of his own country and of Scotland. The writer has often heard him say that he felt greater pleasure in a rushing highland torrent, amid the purple coloured hills and richly wooded valleys of his own country, than among the most awe-inspiring passes, and stupendous mountain heights, that are to be found in the Alps or Pyrenees.

From the following a fair estimate may be made of his power of description—

"*September* 17, 1840. *Between Coblentz and Mayence* — We saw a beautiful, or rather a singular, scene yesterday evening at about five o'clock. We had started from Cologne at four, and were going up the Rhine, when a thunder storm came on. The whole sky became a black or purple colour with vivid flashes of lightning. The wind and rain were so impetuous that we were all driven below. When at last it began to clear, the sun broke out in the west, while everywhere else was as black as midnight. All the nearer objects had a bright yellow glare thrown on them like that from a great fire, contrasting singularly with the black canopy above us. A perfect rainbow of the most beautiful colours suddenly spanned the Rhine, and seemed to rise to an extraordinary height in the heavens. This was succeeded by another and by a third. So that we had a triple rainbow of the most surpassing beauty, and between each arch a mass of iris colours that seemed to have lost their way, erring spirits that had no guide. By and by the black curtain rose more and more from the west, and curling upwards with round masses like drapery disclosed the brilliant sunset. The sunnier Tyrol had a clearness like diamond, and the trees and flowers all the richness of colouring and distinctness of outline we wonder at in Both's landscapes. The clouds after forming masses hanging in the clear æther, like pendants in a Gothic cathedral, gradually rolled away. The sun sank gilding the Drachenfels, and night rapidly set in."

"*September* 23, 1840.—At night we started from Munich for Salzburg, which we reached yesterday evening, after a drive of the most surpassing beauty. You may ask how we could enjoy scenery when we travelled by night—but as you must know Munich is situated in a vast plain, and we managed our time so that the rising sun should see us just entering the great chain of the Tyrolean Alps. And so it did. We were travelling towards the East with the chain of mountains to our right hand. A vast sea of mist hung on the sides of the mountains, and in the valley, and as the sun rose it began to rise in folds like curtains tinged with rainbow colours, and disclosed the mountains successively, each new one a little higher than the preceding. Such a morning and such a view I never saw, for when the whole curtain was drawn we beheld the whole range of the Salzburg Alps, at least one hundred miles long, gilded and glittering in the morning sun, and springing out of a plain with every variety of woodland scenery.

"The road runs along the line of mountains till it reaches the beautiful lake of Chiemsee. It is of great extent. Its shores are flat on one side, but on the other are bounded by the chain of the Tyrolean Alps which for at least fifty miles are reflected on its glassy surface. The day was bright and perfectly calm. The scene reminded me of Lucerne, but the view from the water is much more extended here, and the outlines of the mountains are much more beautiful. At Lucerne one feels confined, but here there is *nothing* to desire. The weather is lovely, and we make a very merry party. I have walked a great deal.

"We went into a little burial-ground to-day, and saw a grave freshly strewed with roses and dahlias.

On looking at the tombstone we found that the occupant of that narrow house had died on this day eighteen years. Is it not a comfort to see such things as this ? "

## VI

POLITICAL VIEWS — CATHOLIC EMANCIPATION —
O'CONNELL—"YOUNG IRELAND" PARTY—THE
GREAT FAMINE—TYPHUS FEVER EPIDEMIC
—MEDICAL CHARITIES BILL

ON the death of his father, in the year 1845,
Stokes was confirmed in the place he had held
as *locum tenens* for two years as Regius Professor of
Medicine in the University of Dublin, a post which
he occupied up to the time of his death.

At no period of his career did he take any active
or public part in the political movements of his
time. His tastes and aptitudes being essentially scientific and literary, he neither sought nor desired to be
identified with any of the great political questions connected with Ireland that so largely exercised the public
mind during his life. Not that he was indifferent to
them; his love for the country was too genuine a one
for him to be so. "To me," he observed, "the real
patriot is he who, in a life of labour and of trial, with

99

integrity, practical wisdom, and far-seeing intelligence, labours onward to no other end but that his country shall rise, and with the honourable and justifiable ambition that, loving her, he may rise with her also."

He felt keenly what he believed were calamitous acts of statesmanship during his time in the Government of Ireland. Among these was the Act for the Disestablishment and Disendowment of the Irish Church. He believed that this would be followed by results the very opposite of those that were anticipated, or said to be anticipated, by the English statesmen then in power, and that it was only another example of the old and discredited policy of confiscation, as carried out previously, in the Governments of Queen Elizabeth, of Cromwell, of James II., and William III., and which had always been attended with complete and disastrous failure. He held strongly the opinion that the best interests not alone of the Church but more particularly of the country would be grievously injured by it. The verdict of history in endorsing or disproving this opinion has yet to be given.

Like his father before him, he had sympathised with the movement for Catholic emancipation, which was at last granted in the year 1829. During the agitation that preceded this event the warm interest that Stokes felt in the efforts of its promoters may be seen in the following passage taken from a letter to his wife, written three months before the passing of the Bill :—

"*January* 15, 1829.—The peoples' minds here are in a great state of political excitement about the Catholic question. The Catholics appear determined to obtain their rights and how the matter may terminate it would be difficult to say. How blind, how infatuated must those men be who persist in refusing them their just rights ! The sword may quell them again and again, the gibbets may be loaded and the scaffolds stream with blood, thousands may be sacrificed, but the voice of millions must be heard at last. Oh ! that those in power would recollect that the system of the sword has now been tried for many hundred years and has produced nothing but strife and misery and heart burning. Oh ! that we could all unite in striving for civil and religious liberty that this fair and lovely land, for which God has done so much and man so little, might put forth its smothered energies which now burst forth only to ruin and destroy."

In the subsequent struggles of O'Connell to promote Repeal of the Union,[1] Stokes only saw much to deplore. When the Association formed to promote this cause was put down by the Government in 1830 the agitation in Dublin was extreme. In the letters written by Stokes at this period we are reminded, however, of the remarks of Mr. Aubrey de Vere, at p. 227 of his Recollections, alluding to the extraordinary elasticity that then as at other times seemed to save the people from utter prostration, " There was a perpetual excitement " ; he writes, " the alternation of the tragic and the comic remained ; the changeful humours held their own." So it was also as Stokes describes it in 1831.

" *January* 20, 1831.—Yesterday O'Connell and most of the agitators were apprehended and held to bail to stand their trial at the next term. This pro-

---

[1] Many anecdotes connected with the Act of the Union Stokes heard in his youth. Of these the writer recollects hearing one which struck him as being very characteristic of the time.

Among those who voted for the Union and who with some eighteen others were rewarded by Peerages or otherwise, were Lords Clare and Clonmell. A county member who also voted on the same side, finding he was unnoticed, waited on the Secretary of State, and in an injured tone complained of neglect. The Secretary answered in the blandest manner : " The Government, Sir, are most anxious to do all it can to assist those who supported it. What is the object of your ambition ? " " Make me aqual to the rest of the blãguards," was the prompt reply of this conscientious legislator. History does not tell if his reasonable request was granted.

ceeding has caused a great excitement here. I was in Dame Street when O'Connell emerged from the Police Office and addressed the people from a drawing-room window. He spoke of the Chamber of Commerce who have united against him, and said he had marked them all and that the mob should have their names. 'What do they want?' he exclaimed. 'They want to see blood flowing in the streets and you butchered by the soldiery.' Soon after this the mob gave three yells for repeal of the Union and then separated. . . . All the moderate people in Ireland are now united against O'Connell and he will soon be put down."

"*February* 1, 1831.—Dublin is now very quiet. O'Connell was to have gone to London yesterday, thinking he had succeeded in having his trial postponed, and accordingly all 'the Trades' turned out to escort him to Kingstown, every man carrying some banner. There were many thousands, but no disturbance resulted. However, just as he was leaving town he got a notice from the Court that his final trial was fixed for Thursday next, so, like the King of France, who marched up the hill with 30,000 men and then marched down again, he went to Kingstown with his escort and then came back again. The medical students have taken up the question here and are divided into two very furious parties. As Dr. Jacob was about to commence his lecture the other day he found a placard on the Repeal lying on his table ; he took no notice of it but the class began to make a great disturbance, clapping and shouting, &c., so he took up the placard and carried it coolly to the other end of the table where he placed it beneath a large skull. Tranquillity was then restored until the end of the lecture when the confusion recommenced. He held up his hand to obtain silence, then with his peculiar tone and gesture said, ' God help you all,' and left the room ! "

" *June* 27, 1833.—There is a bawling fellow under the window just now crying, ' Counsellor O'Connell's most important letter to the People of Ireland to *terrify* them to have the Parliament in Ireland, for the small charge of one halfpenny.' This *is* a most comical country ! "

After O'Connell's death, he felt that when the powerful restraint exercised on the people of Ireland by the great Tribune was withdrawn, the result would be a development of political agitation which would have unfortunate and probably disastrous consequences. What happened afterwards fully justified these gloomy anticipations, and in each agitation commencing with the " Young Ireland " one in 1848, an insurrectionary movement so unhappy in its result, and ending with the " Fenian " disturbance of 1867, and the outrages of the "Invincibles" later on, he saw what he believed were nothing but proofs of a steadily increasing national demoralisation and degradation from which it would take years to recover. Happily he was spared seeing these well-founded anticipations realised in the tragical events—the boycotting, assassinations, cattle mutilations, &c.—in the years immediately preceding and following the murders in the Phœnix Park, of his friend Mr. Burke, and the Chief Secretary, Lord Frederick Cavendish.

But though it is impossible to blind ourselves to the errors the " Young Ireland " party fell into, errors which led to so much disaster to its members as well to their country, we must acknowledge that many of them, and particularly one of their principal leaders, Thomas Davis, were actuated by the highest and purest motives. Thomas Davis knew Ireland so far as in his time she could be known, her history, antiquities, and natural genius. "To amend the habits," as Stokes observed, "as he had awakened the mental energies of his countrymen, was the noble aim of Thomas Davis. To teach them justice, manliness, and reliance on themselves, to supplant vanity on the one hand, and servility on the other, by a just self-appreciation of a proper pride ; to make them sensible that nothing could be had without labour, and nothing enjoyed without prudence. For this, while Providence left him with us, he toiled with faithful and unremitting energy."

This revolutionary movement therefore, which Davis had so much at heart, afforded an example of which history has furnished so many, illustrating the fact that men of high education and refinement, and actuated by the purest and most unselfish motives, may, through a strange lack of prudence and foresight, fail disastrously in the object they had in view, and bring dire calamity not only on themselves, but also on the country they desire to serve.

There were few circumstances that gave Stokes greater concern than the inception of the idea of " Home Rule," and the attempt to carry it out by his friend Isaac Butt, a man of exceptionally great intellectual power, and for whom he always entertained feelings of warm affection and regard. He lost no opportunity of endeavouring to dissuade Butt from a course which he warned him was sure to end in failure, and pointed out that the ultimate consequences would, in all probability, be fraught with peril, and with an increase of disturbance and disaffection throughout the country, the extent of which it would be impossible to estimate. Isaac Butt, however, was not to be dissuaded from carrying out his policy. He rejected all advice and warnings, seeing, or affecting to see, in the movement he advocated, an unfailing panacea for all the alleged woes of Ireland, a means for its regeneration, and a source of national prosperity.

During the Fenian disturbance in 1867–68 and shortly after the escape from Kilmainham Gaol of James Stephens, who was its prime mover and organiser, an incident occurred in Stokes' professional life which is deserving of record, not only from its comical but also from its melancholy aspect, as it shows how deeply a section of the people sympathised with that abortive revolutionary movement. Stokes and his friend Dr. Hatchell, one of the surgeons to his Excellency the Lord-Lieutenant, were summoned to visit professionally the wife of an Irish nobleman who lived on the confines of the counties of Kildare and Dublin. The message was an urgent one, and there being no train available at the time, they both drove down in Stokes' carriage, the distance being

about twenty miles. After seeing and consulting
about the patient, they started on the return journey
at about 10 p.m. The night was extremely dark and
cloudy, not a star to be seen, or a gleam of moonlight.
After proceeding for some two or three miles, to add
to their difficulties, the carriage lamps went out, and
the rain began to pour down in torrents. The road
now became very rough and uneven, and it was soon
obvious that they had got off the main road and into
some intricate byway. They stopped the carriage,
and Hatchell got out and walked on a short distance,
hoping to see some cottage in which information could
be got, and perhaps a guide obtained, to aid them in
their dilemma. For a long time the search was un-
availing, but at last a light was seen coming from a
cottage at a little distance from the road. Hatchell
cautiously advanced to the door, being naturally
anxious as to the probably hostile intentions of a
watchdog, which seemed to regard his appearance with
displeasure. This he evidenced by barking furiously.
Nothing daunted, however, Hatchell advanced and
knocked timidly at the door to which there was no
response, until a second and firmer repetition of the
summons was made. Then the door was opened by
a stalwart, slenderly clad, middle-aged female with dis-

hevelled hair, evidently in a resentful mood at being disturbed at so late an hour. Hatchell explained the situation, and ended by asking for some one to come and show them the way as otherwise they would have to remain out all night. "Show you the way, is it?" replied the virago, "there's no one here to do it, himself is in bed these two days with a stuffin' in his chest, and the boy's away." While Hatchell continued to urge on her to assist them, "himself" appeared on the scene, and he too was obviously indisposed to aid, although offered a pecuniary reward. Then a happy thought occurred to Hatchell. Stooping down he whispered mysteriously into the man's ear. "If you knew who it is that's in the carriage below you'd come quick enough. Don't ask me his name, but I'll tell you this much—it begins with an S!" "Holy Mother of God," said the man, "do you tell me so? Wait a bit and I'll be with you—Patsy," he cried to the son who was snoring peacefully in a corner of the hut, "Git up and we'll show the gentleman the way." Soon they reached the carriage, the father taking his place beside the driver and Patsy walking beside the horses' heads. After proceeding cautiously and slowly for some four or five miles, the carriage stopped, and the man came to the window

and in a low voice said, " Now, yer honor, yer close
to the Kilmainham Road, and sorra thing you have to
do only keep straight on, but turn to the right when
you come to Dooley's and then there's no demur till
yer in the city. I come a bit of a round, as the polis
do often be about here disturbin' the people." He
was then offered a sovereign which was indignantly
refused. Hatchell then said, "Well, boys, you've
done a good job to-night, God save Ireland—We're
not bet yet." " Glory be to God we're not," replied
the man, and the carriage drove on.

At this time the Government had offered a reward
of £2,000 for the apprehension of Stephens.

The years following the Repeal agitation were the
most painful and laborious of Stokes' professional life.
The country was at this time passing through that
mournful period of its history, the Great Famine, a
period which has been often spoken of as if it lasted
but for one year, whereas it continued to recur for
four successive years. The harrowing scenes and
sights in the hospital wards, the long battle with fever
and disease, following on starvation, drew forth all the
courage and manhood of a physician whose large-
hearted sympathy and charity only helped to make
the strain on his system almost past bearing. Nor

did rest come even when the sufferings of the poorer
class at length subsided, and the hospital wards were
somewhat freed, for the scene was only changed to the
homes of the upper classes, and then Stokes often
described his days as passing in "a very whirlwind of
work." To the health of many a good woman and
many a noble lady in the land, these years of tension
proved fatal, and their sufferings were only known to
their physician. The long hours of voluntary duty
in the soup kitchen, the dreary rides on winter days,
carrying saddle-bags filled with meal and bread, over
famine-stricken moors and bogs, to the hovels of the
dying creatures who crawled around the horses' legs
to grasp the offered food, the heart-break and the
misery of it all, told on the constitutions of the
strongest and bravest, and William Stokes was often
heard to say, "If ever a class had its martyrs it was
that of the Irish landowner."

The tragic results of the epidemic of typhus fever
during the years 1842–3 were brought still more
closely home to him when he beheld the havoc
wrought among his medical brethren throughout the
country. During these years typhus fever prevailed
to an appalling extent, and the mortality among
medical men, who were engaged in the Poor Law

service, made him earnestly desire to call the attention of Government to the condition of this class of his medical brethren, and the labours and risks to which they were then exposed. In 1843, when the Medical Charities Bill was brought forward, he and Mr. Cusack united in the effort to procure for these gentlemen some fitting recognition of their labours. They repaired to London to give evidence on the subject before the House of Commons. Both these friends had had to deplore the loss of many of their dearest and most promising pupils, who, after a short experience of country practice, had fallen victims to fever, contracted in discharge of their duties. They pleaded that in all justice the remuneration for attendance on fever hospitals and dispensaries should be fixed at a liberal scale, and that some provision ought to be made for the widows and children of gentlemen who had lost their lives in the public service. They collected statistics which proved that during a period of twenty-five years, the mortality of the medical practitioners of Ireland was 24 per cent., while in most instances the cause of death was typhus fever. They showed that, on the authority of Inspector-General Marshall, the comparative mortality of combatant officers in the army was less than half that amount, being 10¼ per cent. It was little to be wondered at that William Stokes should say, in answer to the Chairman's question regarding the existence of any special risk to the medical officer in Ireland, "Such a number of my pupils have been cut off by typhus fever as to make me feel very uneasy when any of them take a dispensary office in Ireland. I look upon it almost as going into battle." Again he observes : "The medical practitioners in Ireland are placed in a position very different from, and far more serious than that of their brethren in Great Britain. . . . The Irish physician is often exposed to contagion in its most concentrated force when himself under the influences of cold, wet, fatigue, and hunger, as he labours among the poor, passing from hovel to hovel in wild and thinly-populated but extensive districts. He has often to ride for many hours in the worst weather, and at night, enduring great fatigue, while himself a prey to mental as to physical suffering, for if we add to such labour the injurious influence which the knowledge of danger must have on the system of a man feeling that he is struck down by the disease under which he has seen so many sink, and tortured by the thought of leaving a young family unprovided for, we can understand how it happens that the country is so often deprived by death of so many of its best-educated and most devoted servants."

The demand based on these considerations was partially, though *only* partially, successful.

It is not to be wondered at if for a time, after such experiences as are here referred to, we should find traces of melancholy in such letters as the following written to his wife, July 6, 1849:—" . . . I have been too often to blame for low spirits, but sometimes this has arisen from the exhaustion of mind which the multiplicity of my cares and objects produce upon me. I feel myself the centre of a great system, a great machine, complicated and, from its very nature, unresting, and I know that I often fail in the mere physical power to keep it going smoothly. The position I now occupy is no bed of roses, as many who only look on the surface might think, and the last dreadful two years, with their medical and political excitement and national misery, have acted terribly on me. Loving my unhappy country with a love so intense as to be a pain, its miseries and downward progress have lace-rated my very heart, and the 'hope deferred' of seeing some better state of things has had its ordinary effect. When you think of these and other things, and reflect that they have acted on a mind too sensitive and never well regulated, with attachments painfully strong to the perishable, and without clear or active tendencies to the imperishable, you will understand that whenever I do not keep all my blessings strongly before me, I am liable to feel very low. I am not a man of the world in the common sense of the word. I do not love it, and you know that there are very few outside my own dear family in whose society I feel any enjoyment. My profession is on the whole not a depressing one to most men. Nor does it in its ordinary routine depress me. But when a death of importance happens, and that some busy devil within you whispers that had you done something else the result would have been different, and when such an idea from your own weakness becomes fixed, then there is a misery produced which corrodes one's very vitals. The deaths of George Greene, of Curran,[1] of Davis, and of McCullagh, struck me down heavily, for in my treatment of all these cases I feel something to regret. In many such instances the feeling is a mistaken one, for we fret for not having done that of which we had

---

[1] A young physician of great promise, who had been a favourite pupil of Stokes. He died of typhus fever.

no knowledge we ought to have done, and if we do our best, why should we be dissatisfied? But still the feeling is irresistible, and comes over one like a winter cloud. This and the seeing those we love in sickness are the great miseries of the profession of medicine. But when I think of all the blessings God has given me, and His goodness in enabling me to give my children's young hearts the enjoyments which are natural to them, I feel ashamed that I should ever be conquered by melancholy."

There is probably no sadder chapter in the history of Ireland than that which deals with the period of the great famine of 1847 and 1848, and in addition to its sad results—the poverty, starvation, disease, and death, which it carried in its train, it had also the unhappy effect of kindling the latent fires of disaffection and disloyalty, which unhappily are not yet altogether extinguished. The accounts Stokes has given in letters, conversation, and published writings, more especially in connection with famine fever, of which there was such a severe epidemic at that time, illustrate remarkably the descriptive powers he possessed.

As some of our greatest poets and romance writers have at times associated the comic with the tragic element in their works, of which many examples might be cited, so, in the descriptions of some of his experiences acquired during this disastrous period, Stokes would sometimes introduce an account of an incident connected with it, which, by its mirth provoking power, would throw the pathos of his previous account more fully into relief.

M. Soyer, a celebrated chef, had been sent over by the Government, to superintend the manufacture of soup and its distribution to the starving poor from various centres in Dublin. Stokes was accosted one day by a beggar woman, who began to bewail her starvation and her other woes, when he interrupted her by asking why, if her hunger was so extreme, she did not go to secure some of the soup which was being distributed so liberally every day. "Soup, is it, your honour! sure it isn't soup at all." "And what is it, then?" inquired Stokes. "It is nothin', your honour, but a quart of wather biled down to a pint, to make it sthrong!"

During a visit in 1850 to Sir Robert Gore Booth, of Lissadill, Co. Sligo, whose praiseworthy efforts to better the condition of the poor sufferers in that district were well known and fully appreciated at that time, Stokes wrote home as follows :—

# WILLIAM STOKES

"LISSADILL, Co. SLIGO, 1850.

"This is a noble place. The house—a plain and stately structure — stands on a tableland stretching out from the hill side, and it commands the most glorious mountain views on three sides of the building. I think the semicircle of mountains cannot be less than fifty miles in extent, and the forms are as beautiful and varied as any ranges I have seen in Ireland. Many of them are washed by the Atlantic, and so you have, in infinite varieties of combination, all the effects of park and wood, mountain, sea, and lake, wherever you turn. The demesne itself hangs over the sea, and is so extensive that the roads within its bounds are thirty miles in length. The surface is beautifully broken, and the woods, lawns, and rocky banks clothed with wild plants, seem endless. Then this 'happy valley' is, like Mr. Waterton's, a place of refuge for any bird. No nest is to be robbed, no bird killed within its bounds, and such is their appreciation of these advantages that you may see flocks of gold-finches of more than a hundred together. A curious thing happened here yesterday. Two robins flew into the greenhouse which belongs to the clergyman. One of them, it is thought, by beating against the glass, killed itself. The windows were opened to let

the other escape; but no, it would not go, but kept
with its dead comrade fluttering over the dead body,
and caressing it in every way. Sometimes it would
seek to pull it up and place it on its legs, and then,
failing, would show the greatest agitation. Mrs.
Jeffcott, the parson's wife, brought it some crumbs of
bread and immediately it seized on one, and having
first opened the bill of the dead bird, tried to force the
food down its throat. I do not know whether it has
yet left the dead bird. It is thought that the pair
were parent and child.

"This country is full of forts and tumuli, and the
grand tumulus of Knocknaree is to be seen crowning
the top of a mountain beyond Sligo, but I have not
found any antiquities. There is a stump of a Round
Tower and a beautiful cross near this at a place
called Drumcliff. But what gives this place its
greatest charm is that the house is truly the refuge and
hope of all that are poor, sick, and destitute. How
often do I think of Christ's words, 'Well done, good
and faithful servant.'"

It was during this visit at Lissadill that he wrote
the following letter relating to the efforts of his host
during the previous terrible years of Irish famine,

showing that even this tragic period in the history of this country was not without its episodes of fun and humour.

"I have heard a wonderful collection of anecdotes about the famine here. Sir Robert Gore Booth chartered some vessels to send out the people free of expense to America, and when one was on the point of sailing, the names of the emigrants were called over. In one case a ticket had been given for a man and his mother; but when the couple appeared, the mother was found to be a young girl of eighteen. This was his sweetheart, whom he had substituted. 'Hallo,' said Sir Robert, 'who is this one? Is she your mother?' 'No, your honour.' 'Who is she then?' 'She is instead of her.' The girl was ordered on shore, where she set up such a loud wailing that Sir Robert's heart relented, and he asked if they were married. 'No, your honour, the priest would not marry us.' 'Why so?' said Sir Robert. 'Because she wasn't my mother, sir.' There was a priest on board, however, and the couple were shortly afterwards united."

During a visit to the County Westmeath, shortly after the famine years of 1848–49 Stokes heard the following characteristic anecdote of a young cattle jobber who sold a cow to the Protestant clergyman of the parish. The morning after the purchase was effected it was ascertained that the animal was diseased. The jobber was sent for, and told he should return the money, and take away the cow. To this he assented and returned the money. Upon this the clergyman thought proper to give him a lecture on the impropriety of his selling a diseased cow, when he replied, "Don't be angry with me, your riverence. I'm only a lame boy, and have no way of livin' but by strategims!"

## VII

## Pathological Society—Work on Diseases of the Heart and Aorta

SHORTLY after the publication of Stokes' work on diseases of the chest, he took steps to supply a want which had long been felt in the Irish schools of Medicine. The object he had in view was to make provision for the exhibition and permanent record of any specimens of pathological interest that might be met with in the hospitals of Dublin. The result of this movement was the founding and establishment of the Pathological Society of Dublin in 1838. This was the first society of the kind in the United Kingdom. In this effort able assistance was given him by Dr. R. W. Smith, a distinguished pathologist, who subsequently became Professor of Surgery in the University of Dublin. The late Sir Dominic Corrigan

William Stokes, F.R.S.

was also an energetic supporter of the Society from its commencement, and throughout his life a constant contributor to its transactions.

The great object of the Society was the cultivation of pathological anatomy, not merely as a descriptive science, but rather in reference to its more important bearings on the practice of the healing art, the study of morbid anatomy being considered subservient to pathology. It was held that little advantage could be obtained by the description, however minute, of morbid structure without careful attention to symptomatology, combined with a faithful record of the history, diagnosis, and treatment of each case. In fact, the practical application of the truths of pathology was to be the primary object. To attain this end it was considered desirable that such exhibitions should be accompanied by a clear statement of the history, symptoms, diagnosis, and treatment of each case, and that the specimens should be produced as soon as possible after the decease of the patient.

The Society consisted of presidents, vice-presidents, secretaries, a treasurer, council, and ordinary members. Among the original presidents are to be found the names of Abraham Colles, Philip Crampton, Robert Graves, and James Cusack, names of which the profession have good reason to be proud. The two secretaries were William Stokes and Robert William Smith. The latter held the position until the year of his death in 1876 when he was succeeded in the office by Dr. Edward H. Bennett, now Professor of Surgery in Trinity College, Dublin.

The Society, thus formed, soon commanded the support and sympathy of almost every physician and surgeon of any note in Dublin, and many provincial members of the profession in Ireland also joined it. In 1854 the constitution of the Society was altered, only one President was elected annually, and the meetings were held every Saturday afternoon during the winter session in the theatre of the School of Medicine in Trinity College. A large number of the senior students of the various schools of medicine in Dublin enjoyed the privilege and advantage of being allowed to attend these meetings, a privilege which was keenly appreciated. Here they listened with breathless interest to the records of the cases which had furnished the pathological specimens there exhibited, and had an opportunity of inspecting them subsequently, and becoming familiar with the microscopic appearances of many and various forms of pathological change. No discussion was allowed, an arrangement which, although doubtless it would not suit the requirements of the present day, at all events had the advantage of enabling a much larger number of specimens to be exhibited than would otherwise have been possible. At the end of the session a gold medal was awarded to the student who was the author of the best essay on some pathological subject chosen by the Council, and as this prize was regarded as the highest distinction obtainable by a student, the competition for it was always exceptionally keen.

"The object and scope of this society," Dr. Hudson has observed, "might be said to be the reflex of Dr. Stokes' character as a pathologist, not devoted to any school or system, but eclectic, neither regarding morbid anatomy as its first object, but as subsidiary to pathology considered in its widest sense, and embracing the history, symptoms, diagnosis, and treatment of each case of disease submitted to the Society. To this Society, Dr. Stokes, as honorary secretary, devoted for many years such time and labour and made numerous valuable and important communications. These, like his other published works, present the combination of accurate observation and clear insight with mature reflection. No mere observer and recorder of random facts, he seems always to have kept in view the ancient maxim : 'Ars tota in observationibus sed perpendae sunt observationes.'"

To the students who were permitted to attend, the advantages were manifold ; first of all there was the exceptional opportunity they were afforded of studying microscopic pathology, and what perhaps was a still greater advantage, the moral one, derived from witnessing so many distinguished men such as Corrigan, Gordon, Hutton, Mayne, Adams, Banks, McDowel, Law, R. W. Smith, and others whose names were "familiar as household words," not only attending the meetings from beginning to end with praiseworthy regularity, but also taking an active part in the exhibition of morbid specimens, the description of which was always accompanied with a graphic account of the clinical features of the case from which the specimen was obtained.

The writer will ever cherish among the pleasantest reminiscences of his student life the meetings of the Pathological Society, where, in common with the other students, he was so deeply impressed with the earnestness, zeal, and enthusiasm exhibited by so many distinguished members of the

Society, whose communications, as a rule, gave evidence, not only of close and accurate observation, but at times of that eloquence that is ever a product of a genuine love of truth.

About the year 1849–50 Stokes read a paper at the College of Physicians on the light which the study of nervous diseases throws upon what was at that time termed Mesmerism, which has subsequently been termed "Electro Biology," and which, after a lengthened period of occultation, has recently re-appeared with the classical and dignified title of Hypnotism. He shows that the extraordinary epidemics of nervous diseases which were prevalent in Europe for two centuries in the Middle Ages, presented many features similar if not identical with the phenomena observable under mesmeric influence. "In some persons the leading delusion was the belief in heavenly inspiration, while in the larger class, body, soul, mind, and will were held to be under the control of Satan or his demons. The belief in witchcraft was universal, and the disease continued for more than two centuries unchecked by the most sanguinary laws. . . . The intelligence of those affected was exalted, they improvised with extraordinary eloquence and power, and frequently answered in languages supposed to be unknown to them. . . . This condition of the nervous system was communicable from one patient to another just as we see hysteric diseases spread through the wards of an hospital. Madness, convulsions, coma, tetanus, hydrophobia, epilepsy, and hysteria are but manifestations of states of the brain and spinal cord, which we know to be analogous to the conditions of the induced or auto-mesmeric state, and as it has pleased the Great Disposer of all events to spare us from the visitation of these epidemics of madness which occurred in the Middle Ages, it appears to be something worse than folly to reproduce even one of the forms of the malady indirectly, when our doing so can only amuse the vulgar or astonish the ignorant, while we risk the bodily or mental health of one of our fellow-creatures."

In 1854 Stokes delivered a discourse on the Life and Works of "his teacher, colleague, and friend," Graves, who had died the year before of a painful and lingering disease. Paying a tribute to the memory of one, with whom he had so long worked in unison, was indeed to him a labour of love. The early association with Graves had had no small effect in training and moulding the character of Stokes, and the differences in their youthful circumstances and education, only made the one supplement the defects and stimulate the energy of the other. Both were original investigators, and, therefore, successful teachers, for this element of original investigation in a teacher acts in more ways than one: "It leads to the analogic method giving ever to the past a new freshness. In this Graves was pre-eminent ; indeed, his active mind was ever seeking for and finding analogies, and this led him to the discrimination of things similar, and to the assimilation of things dissimilar in a degree seldom surpassed by any medical teacher."

Graves' labours marked, in Stokes' opinion, an era in the history of British Medicine, as they combined in a philosophical eclecticism the lights of the past with those of the present. For his mind, while it mastered the discoveries of modern investigation, remained imbued with the old strength and breadth of view, so characteristic of the fathers of British medicine. In his clinical teaching, the student found the guidance of a mind trained and strengthened by university education, by the study of the exact sciences and of literature ; while in medicine it was so richly stored, that it might be taken as the "exponent of the existing state of the science ; ardent in research, fruitful in discovery, no miser of its wealth, but pouring forth its richness to all who would receive it."

Graves' death at a comparatively early age was keenly felt by Stokes; in him he lost a steadfast and loyal colleague, and one whose learning and exceptional mental powers placed him among the first of the distinguished men of his profession in Ireland.

In 1863 Stokes edited a volume consisting of a collection of Graves' contributions to Medicine and Physiology which had been published in various journals. The work was entitled "Studies in Physiology and Medicine." "Graves was a man," says Sir Henry Acland, "who in a marked degree combined the scientific mind of the physiologist with the intensely practical quickness of the clinical observer." One of his sayings used to be, "When I am dead let my epitaph be, 'He fed fevers.'" His work on clinical medicine, and his remarkable powers as a clinical teacher, will never be forgotten in the history of Medicine in Ireland.

In 1854 Stokes was called upon by the Provost and Senior Fellows of Trinity College to open the Medical Session with an address, a significant fact in the history of the Dublin University, since it implied the increased

energy with which the heads of the University were
turning their attention to the condition of the Medical
and Surgical Schools. It was by Stokes' influence and
through his arguments that the movement in the Dublin
School towards an identical training for the physician
and surgeon was set on foot, and it was to him that
the founding of a diploma in State Medicine in connection with Trinity College, Dublin, was mainly
due. He now set himself, in the first instance, to dis-
pel the factitious and unreasonable division of his profession into medicine and surgery ; "sooner or later,"
he held, " that·this distinction would be obliterated."
" The human constitution," he says, in his opening
address on State Medicine, "is one ; there is no
division of it into a medical and surgical domain ; the
same laws and the same principles apply to the cure of
a fractured bone and the cicatrisation of an internal
ulcer." What he now laboured for, however, was not
the fusion of the two branches of the profession,
though to this he looked forward, as likely both to
further the progress of science and to elevate the
moral and political status of the profession, but rather
identity in the fundamental education of both. Therefore he urged the heads of the University to extend
the benefits of general education to the surgical, as

well as to the medical, student. From an early period, surgery had been excluded, or but feebly recognised, in the academic system of the old Universities. As yet the diploma had not yet been obtained or sought for by any candidate who had not graduated in Arts and Medicine ; and he urged the carrying out of one great reform, which was that full degrees in Surgery should be conferred, having an equal rank with those of Medicine, and requiring that the candidate should have completed his education and graduated in Arts. He observes, "Do not be misled by the opinion that a University education will do nothing more than give you a certain proficiency in Classical Literature, in the study of Logics and Ethics, or in Mathematical or Physical Science. If it does these things for you, you will be great gainers, for there is no one branch of professional life in which these studies will not prove the most signal help to you. But it has other and equally important results ; it enforces respect for the ordinances of religion ; it habituates the mind to the humility of prayer ; it enlarges it by communion with contemporaries who are preparing for their varied walks in life ; and it excites the best ambition, by presenting so many examples of successful exertion ; and lastly, it serves you by increasing your self-respect. . . . You are to support the dignity of a noble profession, therefore your mental powers and your moral perceptions must be cultivated and exalted ; but you are also to be placed in a position, of all others the most fruitful, not only in opportunities of doing wrong to your brother in the dark, but of practising on the credulity of mankind— therefore you must cherish the most delicate sense of honour, and so train yourselves that your conduct shall be based, not so much on the fear of the consequence of wrong, as upon the perfect love of that which is right."

The more than favourable reception which the work on diseases of the chest obtained, and the great repu- tation it gained for the author, acted as a healthy stimulus to him both in writing and clinical teaching. From the time of the publication of the work alluded to, and during the succeeding ten years, his attention had been mainly fixed on the study of the affections of the heart, and a large number of papers were con- tributed by him on this subject to the *Dublin Quarterly Journal of Medical Science*, of which he was formerly the editor, as well as to other professional periodicals. These formed the basis of the work on "Diseases of the Heart and Aorta," one which may be said to be equal in importance and value to the previous one on Diseases of the Chest. The late Professor Lindwurm [1] of Munich translated this work on the Heart, and in his preface he states that the views of the author are in many respects opposed to those then prevalent in Germany, and that now they must decide between the Irish and the German theory, as to the treatment and development of the diseases of the heart. " Thus," he says, " our more modern German works are to a greater or lesser extent only treatises on the physical diagnosis of organic affections of the heart ; Stokes, on the contrary, resists this one-sided tendency which bases the diagnosis solely on physical signs and disregards the all-important vital phenomena ; he lays less weight on the differential diagnosis or lesions of the several valves and on the situation of a sound than on the condition of the heart in general, and especially on the question as to whether a murmur is organic or inorganic, and whether the disease itself is organic or functional, and he devotes his special attention to what were at that day supposed to be functional disturbances of the heart, such as occur in typhus, in anæmia, and in

[1] " Die krankheiten des Herzens und der Aorta von Dr. Wm. Stokes, im auftrage des verfassers aus dem Englischen von Dr. J. Lindwurm." Würzburg, 1855.

nervous conditions of that organ." The method of study which he deplored was one that led men to ignore signs of change continually at work, signs also that may be separate from the original and more important disease " which lies, as it were, hidden by the effects of the disturbance it has itself excited." [1]

Stokes could not form a judgment without viewing his subject all round, as it were, taking in his full grasp the entire phenomena of the case, and it was felt that so large and liberal a spirit in the conception of disease must revolutionise the dogmatic routine of practice. As one of his reviewers says, " The closest, most profound, and reflective study of disease is the characteristic of his work. When face to face with some inexplicable difficulty in the case before him, he reasons from the past circumstances of such a case, and reflects in his examination of its present state, until by long pondering on its unusual phenomena, the solution of the difficulty presents itself in the form

[1] This work was also, in 1858, translated into Italian by Dr. Antonio Longhi (" Malattie del Cuore e dell Aorta di Guglielmo Stokes, Primo traduzione Italiana per cura del Dottore Antonio Longhi." Torino, 1858) ; and, in 1864, into French by Dr. Senac (" Traité des Maladies dur Cœur et de L'Aorte par William Stokes. Ouvrage traduit par le Dr. Senac." Paris, 1864).

of a question, put with the modesty of one who is a searcher into Nature's secrets." [1]

In this work the result of Stokes' clinical observations are embodied, "Observations continued," he observes in the Preface, "almost unremittingly for upwards of a quarter of a century. Yet it is not to be taken as a record of every observation on disease of the heart which may have been noted by me during that time, but rather as expressing the state of opinion produced in my own mind by a long experience, even though I cannot recall many of the facts on which that opinion is founded."

He did not attempt in this instance to produce a comprehensive treatise, but mainly confined himself to dealing with those facts and problems connected with cardiac disease to which, for a lengthened period, he specially had directed his attention. He shows that clinical experience not "unfrequently fails to coincide with the minute descriptions given, and the laws definitely and precisely laid down in some books by the best-known authors, but that complications and difficulties at times arise which not only baffle the inexperienced, but even those of large experience.

[1] See *Dublin Quarterly Journal of Medical Science*, vol. xvii. pp. 124, 135. (1854.)

Those difficulties he believed have arisen from a too exclusive reliance on diagnosis founded solely on physical signs, vital phenomena being overlooked.

In the first chapter, dealing mainly with inflammation of the heart and its membranes, much stress is laid on the character of the pulse in pericarditis, and it is shown that no special condition of pulse can be described as belonging to any form or stage of the disease.

In the treatment of pericarditis it is pointed out that the routine antiphlogistic system of treatment may be carried too far, and may not be devoid of danger, also that there was no analogy between pleurisy and pericarditis, and that the latter is much less capable of bearing any long continuance of depletory measures. He was of opinion that many cases have been lost from overlooking the value of stimulants, and that in some cases the operation of paracentesis may be resorted to with advantage.

The succeeding chapters deal with the organic disease of the organ, of the muscular structures and of fatty degeneration. The sixth chapter deals mainly with the treatment of hypertrophy, either *per se* or associated with valvular disease, and it is contended that, in the latter case, the rules laid down by Sir D. Corrigan should be adopted.

In these chapters is to be found the description of the " Cheyne-Stokes respiration," in connection with fatty degeneration of the heart, a condition observed by Cheyne, although not connected by him with any special cardiac lesion. "A form of respiratory distress, peculiar to this affection, consisting of a period of apparently perfect apnœa, succeeded by feeble and short inspirations, which gradually increase in strength and depth until the respiratory act is carried to the highest pitch of which it seems capable, when the respirations, pursuing a descendant scale, regularly diminish until the commencement of another apnœal period. During the height of the paroxysm the vesicular murmur becomes intensely puerile " (p. 336). In connection with this subject it should be noted that Stokes never committed himself to any theories as to its explanation, nor did he restrict it to the condition in which he had observed its best illustrations.

Here also are to be found in the section on Cardio-therapeutics, the principles first enunciated which are practically identical with those now known as the Schott methods. Stokes observes, "In the present state of our knowledge the adoption of the following principles in the management of a case of incipient fatty disease seems justifiable :—

"We must train the patient gradually but steadily to the giving up of all luxurious habits. He must adopt early hours, and *pursue a system of graduated muscular exercises;* and it will often happen that, after perseverance in this system, the patient will be enabled to take an amount of exercise with pleasure and advantage, which at first was totally impossible, owing to the difficulty of breathing which followed exertion. This treatment by *muscular exercise* is obviously more proper in younger persons than in those advanced in life. The symptoms of debility of the heart are often removable *by a regulated course of gymnastics* or by pedestrian exercise, even in mountainous countries, such as Switzerland, or the Highlands of Scotland or of Ireland. We may often observe in such persons the occurrence of what is commonly known as 'getting the second wind,' that is to say, during the first period of the day, the patient suffers from dyspnœa and palpitation to an extreme degree, but by persevering, without over-exertion, or after a short rest, he can finish his day's work and even ascend high mountains with facility. In those advanced in life, however, as has been remarked, the frequent complications with atheromatous disease of the aorta, and affections of the liver and lungs must make us more cautious in recommending the course now specified" (p. 357).[1]

The use of mercury in cases of a weak, dilated heart in connection with hepatic enlargement and pulmonary disease, is fully discussed, and rules, dietetic and hygienic, such as early hours, muscular exercises, &c., are laid down.

One of the most important chapters in this work is that on the condition of the heart in typhus fever. In this the author points out and discusses exhaustively the remarkable and important changes that the muscular substance of the heart undergoes in this disease. Although it remains doubtful whether these changes may not be due to the commencement of decomposition, or to typhus lesions, the author inclines to the latter theory, his views being opposed to those of Graves on this point, and coinciding with those of Laennec, and also of Louis in reference to the fact that the left ventricle is the portion of the heart primarily affected.

[1] It is worthy of note that Dr. W. Bezly Thorne, the author of the well-known treatise on "The Schott Methods" of treatment, fully acknowledges that this system of Cardio Therapy is evolved from principles "first proclaimed by Stokes" (see Preface, 2nd edition).

The varieties in the phenomena occurring in cases where there were evidences of cardiac softening are ably discussed, as well as the principles of treatment that should guide us in these cases.

In the concluding chapter he discusses displacement, rupture, and deranged action of the heart, also angina pectoris and cardiac neuralgia. He also describes a murmur heard in typhoid fever, to which he gives the name of the "typhoid anæmic murmur." The last two chapters deal with Aneurysm of the Thorax and Abdominal Aorta.

"This volume on the Diseases of the Heart," observes Sir Henry Acland, in his admirable and appreciative sketch of Stokes' life drawn for the New Sydenham Society, "was at once accepted, and since has been received as one of the most acute, graphic, and complete accounts of the clinical aspects of the organ under discussion. It exemplifies in a very remarkable way the several characteristics of Dr. Stokes' mind, at once so purely scientific and so eminently practical. No practitioner can open the volume without feeling it to be a storehouse of knowledge obtained at the bedside. It is sufficient to refer to the table of cases at the close of the volume and to the several summaries at the end of the discussion of the various forms of heart disease to satisfy oneself of the truth of this observation, but two illustrations of his acuteness and care may here be given.

"We read that a murmur with the first sound, under certain circumstances, indicates lesion of the mitral valves. And again, that a murmur with the second sound has this or that value. All this may be very true, but is it always easy to determine which of the sounds is the first, and which the second? Every candid observer must answer this question in the negative. In certain cases of weakened hearts acting rapidly and irregularly, it is often scarcely possible to determine the point. Again, even where the pulsations of the heart are not much increased in rapidity, it sometimes, when a loud murmur exists, becomes difficult to say with which sound the murmur is associated. The murmur may mask not only the sound with which it is properly synchronous, but also that with which it has no connection, so that in some cases even of regularly acting hearts, with a distinct systolic impulse, and the back stroke with the second sound, nothing is to be heard but one loud murmur.

"So great is the difficulty in some cases, that we cannot resist altering our opinions from day to

day as to which is the first and which the second
sound. . . .

"To the inexperienced the detailed descriptions of
such phenomena as the intensification of the sounds
of the pulmonary valves; of constrictive murmurs as
distinguished from non-constrictive; of associations
of different murmurs at the opposite sides of the
heart; of pre-systolic and post-systolic, pre-diastolic
and post-diastolic murmurs, act injuriously—first, by
conveying the idea that the separate existence of these
phenomena is certain, and that their diagnostic value
is established; and secondly, by diverting attention
from the great object, which—it cannot be too often
repeated—is to ascertain if the murmur proceeds from
an organic cause; and again, to determine the vital
and physical state of the cavities of the heart. . . .

"If the question as to the practicability of the
negative diagnosis, with reference to either orifice, be
raised, it appears probable that where a mitral murmur
is manifest, it will be easier to determine the absence
of disease of the aortic valves than to declare the
integrity of the mitral valves in a case of aortic
patency. The experience of each succeeding day
devoted to the study of diseases of the heart will make
us less and less confident in pronouncing as to the

absence of disease in any one orifice, although no
physical sign of such a lesion exist, if there be manifest disease in another, or again, if there be symptoms
of an organic affection of the heart."

## VIII

VISIT TO EDINBURGH—SIR JAMES SIMPSON—NICE—
PHYSICIAN TO THE QUEEN—FELLOWSHIP OF
THE ROYAL SOCIETY—TOUR IN GERMANY

IN 1861, the degree of LL.D. (*honoris causâ*) was
conferred on Stokes by the University of Edinburgh, and few distinctions obtained by him were
more highly appreciated and valued.

During his visit to Edinburgh, to receive the
degree, he was a guest of Professor (afterwards Sir
James) Simpson, a man whose originality, genius,
unceasing industry, and kindliness of heart, won for
him so many friends and admirers. Stokes always felt
it both a privilege and a pleasure to be counted among
them. He describes the ceremony of conferring the
degrees in the following letter to his wife :—

"Next day we assembled at the Hopetoun Rooms
and put on our robes. I had a black gown with a

blue hood and I had just put it on when in walked Lord Brougham. He wore a great coat and a black cravat so deep that it seemed intended to keep his head on. He was then robed in a gown heavy with gold and with a huge gold tassel, and in all my experience I never saw anything so comical. The black cravat, the high collars, the twitching moving nose, and the restless activity of the old man were marvellous. He looked like one of our figures in the charades. Then we formed a long procession, and marched into the hall amid loud cheering. I never heard so noble a speech as Lord Brougham's. When he advanced to deliver it, he took off his cap, and then his grand gown, and looked like an old gladiator stripping for the fight. This action greatly delighted the students. I wish you would read the speech bit by bit, for to go through it all at once would tire you. In the evening we dined and were very pleasant, and I, fortunately, had no speech to make. I might have spoken for the sister Universities, but I allowed the Principal of St. Andrews to answer to the toast. I have been most kindly received by everybody, but yesterday was the crowning day. I forgot to tell you that on Friday evening Dr. Simpson and I went to the drawing-room of the Lord High Commissioner at Holyrood. You never saw such a comical court. There was a screen placed across the long room where the pictures of all the kings are, and at the entrance side we saw a man in a red frock coat who proved to be the representative of Majesty! Then we got into a room about half the size of our drawing-room, filled with ladies and gentlemen. Miss M. and Lady B. were seated on a dilapidated sofa, and Miss M. got up and sang two Scotch songs, 'My Nannie's awa' was one of them.

"Yesterday—Saturday—Henry[1] and I went off with Dr. Simpson at 8 a.m. to Kelso by train, passing Abbotsford and Melrose. We lunched at the doctor's at Kelso, and then went to the mighty ruins of the Abbey. It is one of the finest Romanesque buildings in Scotland. We drove to the valley of the silver Tweed and to Dryburgh Abbey, and from that to Melrose, where we joined the train. How I longed for you and Margaret, for never in so short a space of time did my eyes and heart drink in so much beauty. The day was warm and bright and clear, the wind from the south-west, and now and then a little shower fell after which the sun burst out in glory. The trees had their young leaves out, yet not so far advanced as

---

[1] Stokes' youngest son who subsequently became a member of the Madras Civil Service.

wholly to hide their forms, and they seemed to move and dance in the colour and light of heaven. All along the silver Tweed flowed on through its banks, which now rose into cliffs, now made gentle sweeps through the more open country, its water clear as crystal. Dryburgh Abbey, where Scott lies buried, is so embowered with trees that you do not see it till you are at its walls. Trees around, and trees within, and the sun shining on its lovely fragments of sculptured arches, walls and windows, with the air clear as diamond and soft as gossamer ; the wild cherries one wilderness of blossom, the wild flowers blooming over every carving and mullion in crowns of gold, the thrushes singing, and the murmur of the Tweed heard as a silver accompaniment.

"Here lies Scott—in his own loved Borderland, surrounded in his poet's grave by everything that he loved so much in Nature and place and story.[1] We tore ourselves away. We passed Smalholme Castle, a

[1] The reader will remember the passages in Lockart's "Life of Scott" describing his death and funeral (vol. vii. pp. 394, 396): "It was a beautiful day, so warm that every window was wide open—and so perfectly still that the sound of all others most delicious to his ear, the gentle ripple of the Tweed over its pebbles, was distinctly audible as we knelt around the bed and his eldest son kissed and closed his eyes. The wide enclosure at the Abbey of Dryburgh was thronged with old and young, and when the coffin was taken from the hearse and again laid on the shoulders of the afflicted serving men, one deep sob burst from a thousand lips."

Border keep, and we passed the House of Bemerside ; you know the saying—

> "'Betide, betide, whate'er betide
> The Haig shall be in Bemerside ; '

and in a loop of the Tweed, with woods rising all round, we saw 'Old Melrose,' the original site of the Abbey. The woods, the river and the background of the Eldon Hills,[1] and the valley of Thomas the Rhymer, and hills of Lammermuir, all made a picture that would have delighted you. We next drove to the ruined city of Rosburgh, and came to Melrose Abbey, which we closely examined. Henry was in raptures. I bought two quaighs and I pulled a piece of ivy for you, and then we got back to Edinburgh at 6 o'clock p.m., having passed a day the like of which I may never hope to pass again."

In the following year the first of a long series of sorrows occurred which largely impaired the happiness of his domestic life. This was the death of his daughter, Mrs. J. B. Cowan, at Glasgow, and which was soon followed by that of a favourite nephew.

---

[1] The writer has recently learned from Mrs. A. M. Porter, a Scottish lady, that the popular tradition in connection with these hills is that the "familiar" of the great wizard, Michael Scott, for some reason best known to the ghost, one night split the hills up into their present grotesque shapes.

His wife's health, too, at this time gave cause for great anxiety, and she was ordered to winter on the Riviera.

In the course of the winter, William Stokes visited his family at Nice. In a letter describing his journey he observes, "I had to stay most of Sunday at Toulon as I could not go on, all the places in the diligence being engaged for two days, and only yesterday crossed the Estérel and came here at 8 p.m. The beauty of the innumerable valleys of the Estérel is wonderful. They are clothed with a carpet like an Indian shawl of the finest and most varied colours, produced by the close growth of olives, cork trees, and arbutus, ilex, myrtle, the Mediterranean heath, rosemary, lavender, and many other exquisite plants the names of which I could not tell. Above me were the fantastic summits of the hills, while white patches of snow intermingled with the colours of these wonderful slopes. Nothing in Nature can be more beautiful than these valleys. We went to Cimiez on Thursday and had a grey but pleasant day. The effect of colour produced in the low grounds by the orange groves was very singular. Little frills of gold among the silvery olives. I am delighted with the olives. I first saw them as I came to Toulon, but there they were low and bushy. Their silvery gloss is most singular.

They give one the idea of having been all served out with an infinitesimal dust of eider-down, yet when the sun strikes these they glitter and almost sparkle in the breeze. Here they grow into noble trees and with such wonderfully contorted stems and roots. A kind of lichen grows on them which forms the most beautiful diamond pattern on the dark back of the stems. The lichen is light grey, almost white.

"I have seen nothing here like the valleys of the Estérel. What a place for a water-colour painter ! Everything is there and in such generous abundance and extent that one begins to think that the old world is left behind and you are translated to the very gates of paradise, where

"'that birk grew fair eneuch.'

These valleys, which are innumerable, must be like those we read of in Greece, each forming a picture so that you can take it in as a separate study. They áre like corries in Scotland, those that I saw varying in length from two to five miles, crowned and crested with rocky outlines, in which the ingenuity of nature is brought to its highest power in producing variety and beauty. Up almost to the top, and in every nook

and ravine, grow feathery pines and ash trees, while
the slope stretching from the perpendicular rock far
down to the river's edge forms one carpet of colours,
a close forest, but of shrubs and flowering plants
where you see the arbutus, ilex, olive, and glorious
Mediterannean heath, with here and there a feathery
pine and ash tree, not in dense clumps but in twos and
threes, each group most perfect in beauty. Now and
then you have a glimpse of the blue sea. Try and
imagine all this with the shadows of evening, and the
air loaded with perfume, and you may form some idea
of this marvellous district."

From London, after visiting his wife at Nice :—

" My day in Paris was somewhat dull. It was
snowing. After I left Higgins [1] I went to the Louvre
and wandered through its endless galleries. There
was little light, of course. The collection is, on the
whole, not worthy of France. A portrait by Raffaelle
of a gentleman is the best thing I saw. The Last
Supper I do not think much of, though it is wonderfully drawn and painted, but the head of the Saviour is
feeble and the composition faulty, from its crowding
and anachronisms. I was more interested by the faces
of the people who were painting than by anything

[1] A well-known physician in Paris at that time.

else. The ladies especially. They all seemed to tell some similiar story of talent, and goodness and sorrow. Many of them, I am sure, were working for their bread, at least so I judged from the subjects they were working at, which were not exactly those which a woman would choose if left to her own good instincts."

Shortly after his return from the Continent he received the distinction of being appointed one of the Physicians in Ordinary to Her Majesty the Queen in Ireland. The year following he was elected to the Fellowship of the Royal Society, his proposers being Professor (afterwards Sir George) Stokes, Sir Thomas Watson, Bart., the Earl of Dunraven, Sir Thomas Larcom, Professor Harvey, and Dr., now Sir Henry Acland, Bart., K.C.B.

In the autumn of 1863 two of his sons, Whitley and Henry, went out to India, and the happy circle of his family was still further broken up by illness and death. Stokes was suffering from over-work and great depression till persuaded to take a holiday abroad. The writer of this memoir was then residing at Dresden, and wrote urging him to join him, feeling sure that the art galleries of that city would prove a source of intense pleasure to him. Nor was he disappointed, as the following account of the impression Raffaelle's *chef d'œuvre*, the Madonna di San Sisto, made upon him proves :—

"DRESDEN, *September* 1, 1863.

"We have spent the greater part of two days in the picture gallery here. You will like to know what effect the Madonna of Raphael had on me. I expected—I don't know why—a greater glory or strength of colour. But after gazing a few minutes on this marvellous work I felt how wrong I had been. It is placed in a separate room, which it seems to turn into a sanctuary. No matter how many are present, there is a silence, or, if people speak, it is in the lowest whisper. Involuntarily you walk on the floor on tip-toe, and all uncover the head. The principal colours are purple and red, both so delicate and so harmonised that they give to the whole figure the purity of Heaven. To speak of the expression of the Child! Oh! such love, power, sadness, prophecy, in both faces, as they look into the infinite, and raise you up to be part of it. The whole was a dream of the painter. He saw the Blessed Mother descending to him from Heaven, and so he painted her. In her eyes I could see a strange surprise, a wild but subdued feeling of awe, that she should carry in her bosom the wonderful, the mighty God, the Prince of Peace. She does not look on Him, but into space, and her gait seems rapid, for the purple hood rises full above her, while her naked feet hardly imprint the rolling cloud which floats between her and earth. I feel it presumptuous to write this; for this is a work that 'no matter moulded form of speech' can ever describe. . . . One effect of it is to make you careless about all the other treasures of this vast gallery, in which you have works of Correggio, Titian, Sassoferrato, and hundreds of other great painters. The finest Correggio I ever saw is here, the Entombment of the Virgin. The Infant Christ, Sleeping, by Sassoferrato, is a beautiful picture. Holbein's Madonna is here too, and under it is a beautiful specimen of Van Eyck."

From Dresden the party journeyed to Regensburg, then down the "Royal Danube" to Linz, and from that to Gmünden, crossing the lake under the precipice of the mighty Traunstein, the highest mountain of that splendidly picturesque district. "The air had that softness and almost crystalline clearness that precedes rain, and as we drew towards Ebensee, one side of the lake showed all its glorious and fantastic rocks, forest, hills, and mountains in deep purple, while on the opposite coast to which we were running the woods and grassy slopes in the sunlight were richest green and gold. For more than two hours on our drive to Ischl this scene of wonder was visible, and even after darkness had set in the Traunstein and its court of hills, one more beautiful than the other, could be distinguished. . . . Next morning we started in a *wagen* for Salzburg. The road soon brought us to the lake of Wolfgang, almost surrounded by high snow-capped mountains. The rain cleared off at eleven o'clock, and then came the colours and glittering glory of the scene. The lake of the most delicate blue, then the soft green slopes broken into a thousand forms with the wild forest, and above all the mountains on whose sides seemed to hang long wreaths of vapour-like spirits. One high group rose thousands of feet, and round it like a zone was a complete ring of these magical clouds. On leaving the lake we walked a long way up through the hills among sloping lawns covered with the wild crocus and flowers innumerable, among clear flashing streams wandering from rock to chasm, and washing the feet of cliffs hung with creepers, while below still lay the lake with its mountain background appearing more and more beautiful as we advanced, as if to entice us to stay. . . ."

# IX

MEDICAL EDUCATION—MEDICAL ETHICS—PREVEN-
TIVE MEDICINE—WORK ON FEVER—D.C.L.
OXON.

IN 1861 and the years immediately succeeding
it, Stokes' mind was much occupied with the
subject of Medical Education. In 1861, and again
in 1864 he delivered two addresses, one in the Meath
Hospital and the other in the University of Dublin.
Filled with a sense of the greatness of his profession, he insisted again and again on the means
he deemed best fitted to elevate it in general estimation and in social position, and maintained that
the training of the physician or surgeon should in
no way be inferior to that required for candidates for the Church or Bar. As a basis of
special personal instruction he believed a more sound
and larger general culture was essential. With-

out such culture he insisted that no special
training could bear its fullest fruit, and that
because of the various contrasts now established
between medicine and the whole range of the
sciences. Thus to advance medicine now he
showed that we must call to our aid the sciences
of acoustics, chemistry, and optics. The microscope, he says, " has done for pathological anatomy
what the telescope did for astronomy. For even
as the early shepherds had their Arcturus, their
Orion, and the sweet influences of the Pleiades,
but knew nothing of the infinite glories which
circled above them ; so in the study of structure
the unassisted eye saw but the salient points of
the change, and remained ignorant of all that lay
beyond and below them."

Again, he says, what is above all things needful for
the true physician is the philosophic habit of mind
which a large and liberal education is best fitted to
produce. " Medicine," he said, " is not a handicraft
governed by a fixed rule, or any set of rules that
you can learn by rote. It is not a study of fixed, but
of varying, conditions." Hence he inferred that to
deal with it the mind must have the suppleness
and resource which will enable it to adapt itself

to complex phenomena exhibiting from time to time new characters and varied combinations, and, though no system of education will give the *mens medica* which seems to be a gift of nature, it is evident that a general cultivation of the powers of the mind, and rational habits of observation and induction, must be the best preparation for so important an attainment.

"There is no reason," he adds, "why all branches of human knowledge should not travel and conquer by the same paths. A larger study of ethics may improve the common and the equity law, and with divinity, what light may not come from studies such as have too long been held foreign to it? From the general history of Man, from archæology, from the history of living and extinct creatures of all kinds, the study of the crust of the earth, the science of language, and the laws of latent and manifest life? Thinking on these things, may we not hope reverently, not confidently, that all truths, whether revealed or disclosed, will in God's own time be found to be in unison, and that the proofs of the complete correlation of His works and laws will increase with every year of man's life on earth?"

He dwells on the importance of uniting physiological and medical study with those of divinity
and law, the result of which should be mental
enlargement and protection from charlatanism and
falsehood; medico-legal trials would thus bear a different aspect, parochial and missionary labour would
find a powerful increase to their means of extending
their influences abroad among either the peasantry,
working classes, or uncivilised races of men. The
larger the mental culture, the better the soil which
is to raise the seed of any special science, the richer
will be the crop; the danger or safety of knowledge, in however small degree, is dependant on the
previous condition of the mind that receives it,
and the spirit in which it is accepted and made
use of.

In education three principles should guide our
system—the cultivation of memory, of reasoning, of
observation. The last he shows has been most
neglected. Cultivation of the powers of correct
and minute observation he argues is a paramount
duty, and the study of systematic botany and of
natural history gives the best training that can be
obtained to the powers of observation, though their
practical and immediate use to the student of

medicine may not be apparent; yet the trained intellect, the habits of order and classification resulting from their study, remain after the actual knowledge may be forgotten.

The following observations which have been noted from Stokes' conversations and addresses bear so forcibly on medical education, that a few of them may here be quoted.

1. For instance, "It is with societies of men, as well as with individuals, that which commands scientific respect does not so much depend on the successful teaching of what has already been discovered, as upon the production of original work by the society or individuals."

2. "It is with the living that medicine has to do. The living man must be studied in health as in disease; to the physician or surgeon the sick or wounded man is as the mineral to the geologist, as the star to the astronomer."

3. "Other schools have earned a reputation in physiology and comparative anatomy, and those branches of medicine which are termed theoretic; but the enduring fame of the Dublin contributions to science arises from their essential practicality and truthfulness. They are records of unbiassed observa-

tion made by men originally well educated, and brought up in a practical school."

4. "There can be no greater error than to compel a medical officer to attend to a number of patients beyond that which his mental or physical powers can reach. I speak from experience when I say that no physician or surgeon ought to be called on to attend more than fifty hospital patients daily ; to treat more than this proportion causes exhaustion both of body and mind, and he is rendered unfit to perform duties which of all others require a quiet mind and a vigorous frame."

5. "Additional encouragement must be given to the students to obtain that education which can alone fit them to preserve the social position and rank of their profession, to use the words of a great surgeon, to keep it from degenerating into a trade, and the worst of trades."

6. "In the wards of the hospital the student learns that which cannot be taught in the dissecting-room or in the theatre ; he learns to teach himself to act and to discover. And he does much more. The kindlier feelings of his heart are stirred, and he becomes so trained to works of charity and mercy that their practice is at last a second nature. He acquires

that moral courage by which at the call of duty, or of mercy, which is duty, he learns to despise danger, and to meet death whether it comes by pestilence or by the sword."

7. "Medicine cannot be taught in a purely medical hospital any more than surgery in a purely surgical one."

8. "Medicine is essentially a progressive science, and avails itself of almost every branch of knowledge in its progress. Medicine is an inexact science, but this is no reproach. By this very character it enters into fellowship with the most noble of human inquiries."

9. "We have to do with something which cannot be measured or weighed ; something, too, in which experiment can only be used within narrow bounds ; an element whose nature is yet unknown, fleeting in its action, and every day producing new combinations, not merely new because they were never observed before, but really new as appearing for the first time."

10. "Every connection that can be established between the mathematical and physical sciences and medicine will impart to it more or less of certainty."

11. "Medicine, in its great quality as a practical art, advances in many directions ; of which two may

be indicated as the most important. One is the discovery of new facts, whether relating to physiology, pathology, or therapeutics, each of which, even although its practical bearing be not apparent, enlarges the boundaries of the field of certainty. The second is the application of those new facts, on the one hand, to testing the value of methods long in use; and, on the other, as a guide in the wilderness of the unknown which stretches around us, which we are seeking to explore, and which we hope in time to reclaim."

12. "Do not be misled by the opinion that a university education will do nothing more than give you a certain proficiency in classical literature, in the study of logic and ethics, or in mathematical or physical science. But if it does these things for you, you will be great gainers, for there is no one branch of professional life in which these studies will not prove the most signal helps to you."

13. "There is nothing more difficult than for a man who has been educated in a particular doctrine to free himself from it, even though he has found it to be wrong."

In the year 1869 Stokes planned a work on Medical Ethics, which, unhappily, failing health prevented his ever accomplishing. He published, however, a sketch of the work in the form of an address which he delivered to the students of the Meath Hospital. The subject comprises the principles of honour and moral training which make the profession of medicine a calling for the gentleman and the Christian, and he enlarges on the duties and responsibilities of a profession whose labours are a perpetual exercise of humanity, and in which, to use his own words, " honour is so indispensable and so precious, that he who wants it, or who has soiled it, has no business there."

By the term Medical Ethics is meant the application of ethical principles to medical practice, and it is regretfully pointed out that the subject has hitherto been left outside the formalised systems of education, and it is pointed out how overwhelming are the multiplicity and complexity of the circumstances to which in daily professional practice ethical laws are to be applied, how constantly cases arise in which the selection of the right course of conduct as regards patients and professional brethren is a matter of real difficulty.

He deals with the practical portion of his subject by dividing it under four heads :—

1. As regards the conduct of medical men in connection with Law and State Medicine.

2. As regards the patient.

3. As regards society.

4. As regards the profession to which they belong.

Under the first head he exposes the errors too often committed by medical men when called on to act as witnesses. He shows that their principles should be to give independent opinion without being swayed by partisanship, that no man should ever act as a trained expert to prompt a lawyer in his cross-examination. "Knowledge may be held as property, but it is, as such, held on trust, and that trust, looking at its source, forbids its being used as an article of commerce without some restriction. It is to be employed for the establishment of truth, not for its suppression or mystification. We hold knowledge as under a trust from a higher power, and the greater the value of the trust the more careful should we be that in our hands it be not desecrated."

The following are some of the rules he lays down that should guide the practitioner :—

Practice secrecy, avoid talkativeness, never think aloud in the presence of your patient.

Never, when brought in as a consultant, declare the nature of a disease in the absence of the medical attendant.

Never hold that you have any property in your patient ; be tolerant with the sick in their restless desire to seek other advice ; preserve your independence ; eschew servility.

As regards conduct in society, never allude to your success in practice. Be silent when quackery is discussed. Be tolerant when those who converse on medicine, while ignorant of its foundation, reject legitimate medicine.

Never originate discussion on medical topics in conversation. As regards conduct towards the profession, consider first the patient, second your professional brother, lastly yourself. Be reticent, lest by a casual word upon the previous treatment of the case, you inflict a stab in the dark on your brother's reputation.

When patients come from the country never ignore their local attendant, only correspond with them through him.

Do not communicate any fresh discovery in the case that you may make, without communicating such first to him.

Make no change of treatment without writing your opinion to him. Have no professional quarrel.

Such were some of the rules he would lay down ; but before all things he strove to inculcate forgetfulness of self. To the selfish man medicine is a means, and not, as she should be, a mistress, loved, worshipped, and served for her own sake. He concludes with the words of Hamlet in our conduct towards other men :—

"Use them after your own honour and dignity ; the less they deserve the more merit is in your bounty."

For many years Stokes had long foreseen that the demands of modern civilisation would lead the medical profession into relation with the Government of the country. His views as to the necessity for joint action of the state and the profession were in some degree carried into effect by the creation of the General Medical Council, of which Stokes was nominated the Crown Representative for Ireland in 1858. He found in Sir Henry Acland, who for many years presided over the Council, and whose warm and long-tried friendship was the support and solace of his declining years, his best adviser in the all-important questions that arose in connection with sanitary science.

As has been already stated (see p. 131), it was mainly due to the exertions and influence of

William Stokes that the University of Dublin established in 1871 the Diploma in State Medicine for
such medical graduates as have made a special study
of the extensive group of subjects included under the
name of Preventive Medicine. But State Medicine
included forensic, psychological, as well as preventive
medicine, and his first public utterance on this
question was in his discourse on medical ethics in
1869. Then in 1871 he announces that the University of Dublin had instituted the Diploma in State
Medicine, the candidate for which must not only be
fully qualified in arts and medicine, but will be liable
to be examined in pathology and in vital and sanitary
statistics, engineering chemistry, natural philosophy,
meteorology, and forensic medicine. But, as has
been truly observed by Dr. Bernard, of Derry, "long
before Preventive Medicine came to the front, Stokes'
ideas were well known and appreciated, and that the
main object of his labours was to promote preventive
as distinguished from curative medicine."

State medicine is divisible under two heads, legal
and preventive, but the questions of medical juris-
prudence contained in the one are passed over, and he
directs attention mainly to the question of sanitary
measures comprised in the other.

Preventive medicine is to be distinguished from curative as dealing with causes, while the other deals with effects which may become causes. But he never ceases to impress upon his hearers that he speaks of causes only in a secondary sense. The true origin of disease is not ascertainable. The origin of physical as of moral disease remains a mystery ; it is still a question whether disease results from any original, or natural law of our being, or is its preordination by the Almighty a punishment for the neglect of His laws ? It is a breach of the laws of Nature, a perverted life process, an encroachment on the Divine plan interfering with that *vis medicatrix* which often by a mere influence of time and rest,

> " Hath an operation more divine
> Than breath or pen can give expression to,"

and which may reduce these perversions back again to the physiological limits when health may be restored.

But he shows that the practical question for the promoters of State medicine, is not as to the first origin of disease, but as to " how public health is to be best maintained so as to escape the influences which deteriorate it and prevent progressive physical and moral decay, not of the individual man alone, but of communities of men ? To ascertain, to proclaim, and in God's own time to clear away the lets and hindrances which everywhere prevail to the working out of the laws of the Almighty for the well-being and the happiness of His creatures ; laws which are every day lost sight of through that public ignorance, immorality, and selfishness which, making all things subservient to the lust for gold, constitute the real danger to these countries. Think," he adds, " of the millions of our fellow-men, brethren, subjects of the same Crown at home, or on the burning plains of India, contending miserably with, or yielding to the multiplied evils of degradation, and consequently untimely death, from whom the ignorance of their rulers as well as of themselves, keeps the light of knowledge, and you will admit that it is a noble object for those who dwell in, and who govern these homes of science, our ancient teaching Universities, to prepare and send out over the world their disciplined and devoted soldiers of science and ethics, endowed with the highest academical and social rank, to contend with and abate those moral and physical evils, the growth of ages, the offspring of ignorance, which have so long afflicted and retarded mankind ! "

One of the outcomes of Stokes' efforts in the promotion of the study of preventive medicine was the establishment of the Dublin Sanitary Association. In the theatre of the Royal Dublin Society he delivered one of a series of lectures on sanitary science, under the auspices of the Dublin Sanitary Association. In his discourse he dealt mainly with the causes and origin of epidemic disease, the laws of contagion, sanitary engineering, and sanitary law. The lecture was delivered with much eloquence and pathos, and made a very deep impression on his audience. It was largely attended ; all present knew they were listening to one who by fifty years' labour among the poor of Dublin was well fitted to instruct them in dealing with these vital questions. " Here," he said, "we have no subjects for oratory even if we had the power to use it. But we are here to tell you that which we know, and which must be known and thought upon, and to bid the victims of misery, physical degradation, and the unsparing pestilence, plead for themselves.

> " 'Show you dead Cæsar's wounds,
> Poor, poor dumb mouths,
> And bid them speak for me.' "

In 1864, shortly after the death of his friend and colleague, Mr. Josiah Smyly, he delivered an address in the Meath Hospital on the life and work of that eminent and successful surgeon. The discourse was full of the sympathy, good feeling, and generous appreciation of a loyal colleague.

In the following year he was invited to deliver the address in medicine at the annual meeting of the British Medical Association held in Leamington, and chose as his subject, the much-disputed topic of the "Change of Type in Disease." The views held by Alison, Christison, Watson, Graves, and many others, that the character or type of many affections did undergo change in their time, change which necessitated a revolution in treatment, from a system of venesection and almost starvation to the exhibition of stimulants and the careful use of nutriment, found a strong supporter in William Stokes. "This change," he observes, "has given rise to the charge against our predecessors and teachers that they were bad practitioners, ignorant of true pathology, little better than blind followers of traditional error. Not only has their power of observation been questioned, but their morality and honour have been assailed, for it has been suggested that the doctrine of change of type was an invention to cloak their former errors." The existence of such charges, and the fact that writers such as Professor Bennett, of Edinburgh, and Dr. Markham, who held that the doctrine of change of type was untenable, were at variance with Stokes' convictions and experience, induced him to state his views on the subject in this remarkable discourse.

"Medicine," he says, "like other professions involving human interests, has been continually assailed from without and harmlessly.  Attacks on her honour proceeding from her own children, no matter what amount of ability may be shown, while they inflict a deeper wound ever recoil upon their authors.  This has been well exemplified in the case of Paracelsus, who burned the books of the Greek, Roman, and Arabian physicians."

Impelled by a chivalrous desire to defend the great fathers of medicine, his teachers and predecessors in his art, from the charge of empiricism and ignorance, he shows what was the experience of his predecessors and then he adds his own testimony to that of the teachers mentioned above.  He had been thirty years in practice, and had witnessed this change in the character or type of fever in Ireland from 1820 to 1830, and from that to 1860.  As Secretary to the Pathological Society of Ireland he had examined many thousand specimens of diseased structure, and, in cases of acute disease, the anatomical changes were very different from these commonly met with in the early periods of his career, that is from 1820 to 1830. At this time the specimens as a rule all showed "appearances indicative of a less degree of pathological activity." The differences in the pathological changes in certain acute inflammatory affections observed during the period above specified and that following it were best illustrated in pneumonia; "the redness, firmness, compactness, and defined boundary of the solidified lung was seldom seen, and that state of dryness, and vivid scarlet injection, to which I ventured to give the name of the first stage of pneumonia, became very rare. In place of these characters we had a condition more approaching to splenisation, the affected parts purple not bright red; friable not firm; moist not dry; and the whole looking more like the result of diffuse than of energetic and concentrated inflammation; or we had another form, to which Dr. Corrigan has given the name of blue pneumonia, in which the structure resembled that of a carnified lung which had been steeped in venous blood."

At the same time he observed considerable alteration in the pathological character of many of the inflammations of the serous membranes, "the high arterial injection, the dryness of the surface, the free production, close adhesion and firm structure of the false membranes, in acute affections of the arachnoid, pericardium, pleura, and peritoneum, with which we were so familiar before the time in question, ceased in a great measure to make their appearance. The exudations were more or less hæmorrhagic, the effused lymph lying like a pasty covering rather than a close and firm investment; it was thin, ill-defined, and more or less transparent. In many of such cases, during the disease, as the late Dr. Mayne has shown in his memoir on pericarditis, friction sounds were never presented. Serous or sero-fibrinous effusions tinged with colouring matter replaced the old results of sthenic inflammation, and all tallied exactly with the change in the vital character of the disease."

The writer is quite aware that these views of Stokes, as regards the alleged change of type in inflammatory and febrile affections, are not in harmony with those held and taught by the majority of pathologists in the present day. But still he feels it is hard to realise the possibility of so complete an error in this respect being made by those who were possessed of such exceptional powers of close and accurate observation and large experience as the illustrious physicians already mentioned, and whose views are still accepted by many living acknowledged authorities.

The writer feels it would be inappropriate for him to make any dogmatic assertion on this subject, it being one that lies outside his path of study and investigation; but, having regard to his own clinical experience in surgery, he sees no justification for the almost contemptuous rejection of the change of type theory by some pathologists and physicians of the present time. Graves, in his "Clinical Medicine," speaking of the variations in scarlatina and other diseases, as observed by himself and others, remarks that they "establish the real existence of a change in the constitution of diseases." Some forms of so-called surgical disease, formerly familiar to the writer in his student days, have disappeared or are observed but rarely and in a mitigated form. He alludes more particularly to the extensive and violently acute forms of syphilitic phagadœna, such as have been described so graphically and vividly by Mr. Wallace, formerly surgeon to Jervis Street Hospital, phlegmonoid erysipelas, and acute gangrene, cases of which, during his student days, were too frequently the subjects of observation and treatment in the surgical wards of the Meath and Richmond Hospitals; also instances of those often fatal cases of anthrax or carbuncle and cancrum oris, the latter relentlessly sparing no structure, and usually uninfluenced by treatment however bold, rapidly pursuing its fatal career till checked by death alone. Of such cases little conception can now be formed by the surgical student, were it not for the descriptions and illustrations of them which happily still survive. Such cases he never sees now.

As, therefore, these changes in the character or type of these so-called "surgical" diseases unquestionably have taken place during the past twenty-five years, the writer sees no reason to suppose that during William Stokes' professional career, changes of type may not have occurred in the diseases to which he devoted special attention.

Bacteriology has unquestionably largely revolutionised the views held formerly as regards the pathology of fever; and doubtless had Stokes and many of his distinguished contemporaries lived in the present day, many of the views which they held and defended with so much subtlety and ingenuity, would probably have been materially modified. Yet, still, as regards change of type, there seems to the writer that as yet no distinct proof has been given that the theory is wholly untenable. There seems to him no reason why, with improved conditions of life, there may not be corresponding changes in the character and phenomena of disease, due possibly to the conditions of life, among the poorer classes especially, having undergone distinct improvement during the past twenty-five years. That this change for the better has taken place there can be little doubt; the question, therefore, as to the truth or otherwise of the change of type theory must at all events still be regarded as " not proven," and consequently in the present state of our knowledge, undeserving of the opposition it has met with at the hands of many.

The change of type theory is strongly maintained in Stokes' last published work, " Lectures on Fever delivered in the Theatre of the Meath Hospital " 1874,[1] as well as the question of separate identity of typhus and typhoid fevers, both being subject, though in varying degrees, to the law of periodicity. He held that these forms, though doubtless presenting striking differences, yet were differences rather of species than of genera. The doctrine of essentiality in fever was also one on which Stokes based his views as regards the nature of fever; and here again he was strongly supported by such accurate observers as Alison,

[1] This work was edited by Dr. Stokes' pupil and friend, Dr. J. W. Moore, physician to the Meath Hospital, whose recently published work on fever has placed him in the front rank among authorities on this subject.

Christison, and Graves, who coincided in these doctrines. But there seems to be little doubt that, as Sir William Gairdner has said, "by disowning the essential difference between typhus and enteric and between both of these and relapsing fever they got into a wrong groove." He has raised the question whether Christison and the other advocates of the identity doctrine would have held by it after the discovery of Obermeier's Spirillum, or Eberth's Bacillus Typhosus. There can be little doubt that they would have promptly abandoned it. "But," Sir William Gairdner observes, "although Murchison has rightly shown the misconception which arose out of this doctrine as regards the men of the olden time, yet that does not quite dispose of their authority as regards 'change of type' in general, and I am content to occupy a position of suspense in some respects as regards the main question."

From these considerations it would seem unphilosophical to wholly accept, or entirely reject, the theory that a change of type has taken place in the character of fever.

It must at all events be admitted that if we regard the clinical aspect or symptomatology alone of the continued fevers much may be said in favour of the view that they are species rather than distinct genera ; but from an etiological standpoint such a doctrine is no longer tenable in the light of modern bacteriological research and discovery.

It seems unnecessary to discuss the doctrine of " essentiality " in fever. The birth and development of bacteriological science which has taken place of late years renders it so. This, however, cannot be said of the doctrine that both the typhus and enteric forms of fever are subject to the law of periodicity, a doctrine which leads Stokes to make in these lectures on fever " numerous observations of the highest importance," as was observed by the author of the appreciative obituary notice of Stokes which appeared in the *Birmingham Medical Review* (April, 1878). "We are not permitted," he remarks, "to exclude many other diseases from the operation of this law. If there is anything established in medicine it is that all acute diseases, when not subjected to interference, tend to terminate within a more or less definite period. The rhythmic course of pneumonia is universally recognised, and is scarcely less marked than in relapsing fever or typhus, and more marked than in many examples of enteric fever."

No clinical physician of experience can now deny the existence of the law of periodicity of which Stokes speaks. It has been reserved for modern medical and pathological research to explain that law. Can we doubt that the periodic ending of an acute infective disease means that the battle is over and that victory rests with the defensive forces of the system in their struggle with the invading specific micro-organisms, or the poisonous products to which they in their life and death have given rise.

But however opinions may differ as to Stokes' theoretical views of the nature of fever, no one will fail to recognise, as the author above quoted observes, "the matchless clinical acumen displayed in these lectures." Four of these are devoted to the consideration of the heart in fever, three to the nervous, and one to the hysterical complications of fever. Of these probably the latter is the one that has been considered of the highest import.

It may be said in conclusion that in this work theoretical views are embodied some of which appear not to be in harmony with modern pathological research ; but as a "set off" against this, we have a record extending over nearly half a century of accurately noted clinical experiences of fever, such as to entitle it to a foremost place among the classical works on the subject.

In 1865 the degree of D.C.L. *(hon. causâ)* was conferred on Stokes by the University of Oxford at the Encænia of June 21st. Among the other recipients of this decree at the same time were Professor (afterwards Sir Robert) Christison, of Edinburgh ; Sir Henry Sumner Maine, K.C.S.I., Cambridge ; Sir Hugh Rose, formerly Commander-in-chief in India ; and Lord Lyons, Her Majesty's Minister in Washington.

# X

## Visit of British Medical Association to Dublin—Archæological Tour

THE British Medical Association, the main objects of which have been truthfully stated to be "the advancement of medical science, and the elevation of the social condition of our profession," had, ever since its inception by Sir Charles Hastings, commanded the sympathy and goodwill of Stokes. It was, therefore, a source of unalloyed satisfaction to him to learn that its annual meeting was to be held in Dublin during the autumn of 1867. The meeting proved a remarkable one, from the number of distinguished professional men who attended it, and from the fact that it was the first time the association was hospitably received by a University. It may be said that at that meeting the first of these great advances was made, which have since culminated in the result that the Association is now, from the number and character of its members, a power in the State, and the largest professional brotherhood that exists. Stokes was President on this occasion, and in his inaugural address he pointed out its objects, the effects of its operation not only as a scientific body, but as a means of promoting friendly feelings by the personal interchanges of kindly offices, "a means of getting rid of prejudices, and of neutralising those corporate jealousies, so long the bane of our profession." Thus they not merely hoped, but foresaw that the time would come when that profession would be bound together as a united body, looking ever upwards, and strong in mutual respect and mutual confidences. The topic mainly dealt with in this address was that which had filled his thoughts for the last four years, and which we have already enlarged on at page 171—that is, State Medicine. The establishment of a Diploma in State Medicine in the University of Dublin was a scheme he had long striven to promote, the achievement of which may be held to be one of the greatest in his life as man. The example thus shown was quickly followed by the sister Universities of Oxford and

Cambridge. He also dwelt on the importance of a large and liberal education as the best preparation for special training, on the desirability of investigating the laws of epidemics, and the placing of therapeutics on a more scientific basis. He concluded the address with the following words :—

" The history of Ireland is a singular one. More than a thousand years ago she was a centre of Christianity in Western Europe. Often defeated, though not conquered by the Northman, torn by internecine war and exhausted by fruitless contests with England, she is at last united with her; and the two countries are now beginning to know one another better, and to excuse or to forget what was wrong on either side, and to know and estimate that which was right. According to the use that was made of them, and according to the amount of truth or untruth that may be in them, the traditions of the past may be fruitful in evil or in good. But with the advance of education, of intelligence, and above all of intercommunication, old ignorances, old prejudices, old memories of wrong and forgetfulness of right, will fade away. This visit will hasten the time when the crown of our loved Sovereign will surround and embrace in its golden circle an united and happy people. That day is coming ; and therefore it is clear that this meeting has a national as well as a scientific importance which recommends it to all loyal and all right-thinking men."

This meeting of the Association will always be regarded as one of the most memorable in its annals, not only from the number of illustrious men who attended it—Syme, Simpson, Acland, Hughes Bennett, Teale, Sibson, Rumsey, Lockhart Clarke, Lister, Spencer Wells, Thompson, and many others—but also from the exceptionally brilliant addresses in medicine and surgery that were delivered by Sir Dominic Corrigan and Professor R. W. Smith. The halls of Trinity College " rarely heard orations more weighty, more elevated in tone or more framed in noble aspirations." The writer here quoted (*British Medical Journal*, August 17, 1867) further remarks in reference to Professor Smith's address, that it was delivered " with weighty, thoughtful and deep-toned fervour, fraught with a generous earnestness of mind, a love of the ancient worthies of our literature, a critical and observant appreciation of clinical facts, and above all a high canon of ethical judgment which aroused the learned and numerous auditors to a degree of enthusiasm which is rarely witnessed, and which was expressed not only in frequent and hearty applause, but in the rapt, deepening attention with which every sentence was followed, and the climax of enthusiastic cheering with which the peroration of the orator was greeted."

Another most important and remarkable address delivered at this meeting was that of Dr. Rumsey on preventive medicine. It may, in truth, be stated that one of the greatest and most far-reaching results of the meeting was the impulse given in this address to the study of that branch of medical science, in which we have shown that Stokes took so deep and absorbing an interest.

At the conclusion of this meeting Stokes joined his friend the Earl of Dunraven and his party in an archæological tour through Galway, Sligo, and Mayo, visiting the islands along the coast. From the date of Petrie's death he had encouraged Lord Dunraven to complete the work too long left unfinished, on Irish Ecclesiastical Architecture.[1] In a letter to his eldest son [2] Stokes observes :—

[1] This was not published in Lord Dunraven's lifetime. He left the completion of it to Miss Margaret Stokes, who brought out the work in 1875.

[2] Whitley Stokes, LL.D., D.C.L. Oxon, C.S.I.E.

"We spent nine days in the island of Arran. I
found it very hard work, from early morning till
night trudging over the limestone rocks and throw-
ing down dry stone walls every hundred yards. But
we have done great work, and we have measured,
drawn, and photographed almost every object of
interest in the three islands. I wish you had seen
the group of natives that surrounded us in the great
pagan fort on the middle island of Arran ; nearly a
hundred women and girls, all in their bright red
dresses, sitting in a great circle round us, some at
the base and some at the top of the great wall.
Then we made a young man sing to us, and it was
delightful to see how all the people enjoyed the
song—an interminable Irish chant, but very beautiful in its way. We are now waiting here at Letterfrack for the sea to go down, to allow us to land
on High Island, where you have to jump on to the
cliff with the rise of the wave. How our photo·
graphic apparatus is to be got on shore, seems a
puzzle."

The following year, on his wife's account, he
accepted the kind offer of Lord Dunraven, who
lent him his cottage on the island of Garinish, in
Kenmare Bay, where he trusted that in the mild

climate of the South of Ireland she might find relief
from the suffering caused by the pulmonary malady
from which for so long a time she had been suffering.
Here he followed her in the autumn, and, joined by
Lord Dunraven and Mr. Mercer, they proceeded
to examine and photograph the antiquities of Kerry
as they had done those of Galway, Mayo, and Sligo
the year before. A detailed account of the places
visited on this occasion is given in Lord Dunraven's
" Notes on Irish Architecture" (pp. 1–92).

On another occasion, while engaged during one
of his annual holiday excursions, in investigating the
antiquities of the South of Ireland, he witnessed a
sunset of exceptional beauty from Sybil Head. The
following picture of which, given in a letter to
Carleton, the Irish novelist, is an example of his
descriptive power : " Over the surface of the great
Atlantic, and at least a thousand feet beneath where
we stood, lay a boundless extent of mist or vapour,
which, before it became tinged by the sun's rays,
had assumed the appearance of an open champaign
country, divided, as it were, into large fields, spacious
highways, broad pastoral plains, and extensive
meadows. Gradually, however, this scene changed,
and as the sun began to sink in the far distance,

his sloping beams caught the upper portions of this beautiful vapour, and coloured them with an exquisite variety of the richest hues, each portion assuming a different tinge, in consequence of its position with regard to the sun. The effect of these higher parts, thus lit up into glowing and varied splendour, as contrasted with the calm, broad reaches of wonderful country which lay under them, was inconceivably fine. Thus elevated, they looked like towers of gold and precious stones, shining under the evening sun, in some enchanted land.

"A more wonderful effect was still to come. As the sun went down into the sea the whole expanse by degrees kindled into one great flood of prismatic light, glowing in the richest and most gorgeous colours, all of which now blazed with the deep effulgence of what seemed his last glow.

"Then a third change came on the scene.

"All at once the sun's disc dipped into the ocean, where it had nearly disappeared, leaving on this cloud scenery, a golden haze, rich, warm, and transparent. But this was illusion, for the sun, which had only set in a deceptive horizon, reappeared in a few moments, thus literally seeming to rise again. He now shone for a brief period in mild and cloudless effulgence.

"The cliff from which we contemplated this scene was covered with lichens and mosses of various colours. It stood out mighty and stupendous, facing the crimson sun, whose deep empurpled light touched the whole magnificent mass with colour. Then the sun finally sank, and two eagles shot out far below us from the side of the cliff, and rose circling and wheeling round till they disappeared in the darkness. The rich colour faded away, the deep-tinted fires grew fainter and fainter, the ideal world vanished, darkness succeeded, the winds, as it were, leaped into motion, the mighty waters began to heave, and there remained before us nothing but the desert bosom of the dark Atlantic."

It has been already mentioned that outside his professional pursuits there was nothing that was a greater source of interest or pleasure to Stokes than the study of archæology. Many of his well-earned vacations were spent visiting, in company of one or more of his friends, some of the Early Christian or pre-Christian structures which are to be found in such numbers in some of the remoter districts of Ireland. On one of these annual holidays in the Co. Kerry, being anxious to make an expedition into a wild, mountainous region, four ponies were hired for the party from a farmer living in a village close to where Stokes was residing. When the day arrived on which they purposed making the excursion, no ponies were forthcoming, and on inquiries being made at the village to ascertain the reason of this, the man from whom the ponies had been hired, observed : " Ach ! yer honour, an onconvanient auld divil died here yesterday, and all the ponies is gone to the funeral ! "

*Apropos* of funerals, it was related by Stokes that a man observed of a friend of his who had got his own coffin made, " I think it was very presumptuous of him to do such a thing." " How so ?" said the other. "Because," he replied, " how could he know that he'd ever live to make use of it ! "

Another subject that always interested Stokes on these expeditions was learning some of the popular remedies on which the peasantry had chief reliance in the treatment of various maladies. Some of them are curious if not efficient.

The following account of a method of treatment for epilepsy will be regarded as an interesting, though somewhat heroic addition to our therapeutic resources for that malady, and at one time was said to be of high repute in the southern part of the Co. Kerry.

Mr. Bland, of Derriquin Castle, met one of his tenants, "Well John," said he, "how is the boy?"

"He's well! sir."

"How did you cure him?"

"I deluded him to your honour's bog."

"And what did you do to him there?"

"I drownded him your honour."

"How was that?"

"I brought him to the edge of your honour's bog-hole and threw him in suddint, and lept down upon him, and held him under the water till the last bubble was out of him, and he never since had a return of the complaint, glory be to God!"

## XI

## Meeting at Oxford—Presidency of the Royal Irish Academy

THE year following the Dublin meeting of the Association the University of Oxford followed the example set them by the sister University in Ireland, and received the Association at its annual meeting. Sir Henry Acland, Bart. (then Dr. Acland), presided, with his wonted dignity, courtesy, and geniality.

The following valedictory address was delivered by Stokes, the outgoing President, on that occasion :—

" To be chosen to preside over a society of three thousand educated gentlemen, all zealous for the advancement of human knowledge, many of them distinguished in the paths of literature and science, and not a few of them practical doers of Christ's work upon earth, is a distinction of which any man might be proud, and for which any man should be thankful. For, though the place of meeting influences the selection of President, the character of him who is to preside influences, at least among other things, the choice of place of meeting. Here, for the second time, you meet in Oxford, the heart of England, whose history is that of the country, the free, the enlightened, the religious—the conqueror in the arts of peace and war.

" Let me, before bidding you farewell, say a few words as to the future of this Society—now the most numerous body working for the benefit of science in the world, and which will doubtless attain to larger dimensions. So far, we have been an united body, which is to be attributed to our federal constitution, with independent local action, and a representative and imperial executive. How long this strength-giving union may last, no man can predict ; nor, on the other hand, can any man say to what an amount of influence for good this Association may attain. But it is plain that its durability and usefulness will depend on its being made the instrument for public good, rather than the machinery to advance the immediate worldly interests of the profession. And every one of us must lay it to heart, that a great issue rests within his hands.

The man among us, who, by his unselfish labour, adds one useful fact to the storehouse of medical knowledge, does more to advance its material interests, than if he had spent a life in the pursuit of medical politics. Far be it for me to say that there are not great wrongs to be redressed. It is impossible, in any country, that evils of custom and of administration, private wrongs, corporate shortcomings, hard dealings, unfair competition, and scanty remuneration for public and private services, should not occur. But these evils being admitted how are they to be lessened, if not removed? Is it by public agitation and remonstrance addressed to deaf or unwilling ears? Is it by the demand for class legislation? or is it, by the efforts of one and all, to place medicine in the hierarchy of the sciences—in the vanguard of human progress ; eliminating every influence that can lower it, every day more and more developing the professional principle, while we foster all things that relate to its moral, literary, and scientific character? When this becomes our rule of action, then begins the real reform of all those things at which we fret and chafe. Then will medicine have its due weight in the councils of the country. There is no royal road to this consummation. On the one hand, the liberal

education of the public must advance, and the introduction of the physical sciences in the arts courses of
the Universities must give the death-blow to empiricism ; and, on the other, the education of ourselves
must extend its foundations, and we should trust far
less to the special, than to the general training of the
mind.    When medicine is in a position to command
respect, be sure that its reward will be proportionally
increased, and its status elevated.    In the history of
the human race, three objects of man's solicitude may
be indicated : first, his future state ; next, his worldly
interests ; and lastly, his health.    And so the professions which deal with these considerations have
been relatively placed : first, that of divinity ; next,
that of law or government ; and, as man loves gold
more than life, the last is medicine.    But, with the
progress of society, a juster balance will obtain,
conditionally that we work in the right direction,
and make ourselves worthy to take a share in its
government, not by coercive curricula of education,
not by overloaded examinations in special knowledge,
which are, in comparison to a large mental training,
almost valueless ; but by seeing to the moral and
religious cultivation, and the general intellectual
advancement of the student.    Doubtless, such a

revolution, which, could men only read the signs of
the times, is slowly though surely coming, will lessen
the number of a certain order of candidates for license
to practise.   Doubtless, also, while the funds of special
corporations will be diminished, University education
will be extended ; and the whole character of medicine will be changed, greatly to the advantage of
its social position in the country, and the interests
of science and the public at large.

   " These principles have, from the first, influenced
the General Medical Council, whose efforts have been
so much directed to the promotion of general education, and who, while administering an imperfect law
to the best of their ability, and persevering in what
they believe to be the right course, have been exposed
to depreciating observations.   As every one knows,
the Council has no direct coercive powers in the
matter of education, and I believe that, at least as yet,
it is better that it should not have such powers ; but I
know that I speak the sentiments of the existing
members of that body, whether its constitution be, or
be not changed, when I say that they look to the
profession at large for moral support and for counsel.

   " Our being invited to this metropolis of ancient and
modern British thought, which, with its sister Univer-

sities of Cambridge and of Dublin, has so effectually subserved the real interests of medicine, is a graceful compliment to the Association, and an evidence that this great University will still more foster the cause of medical science.

" Putting aside the success of your labours at Dublin, in a scientific point of view, your meeting of last year deserves a long remembrance. It was the first occasion on which the members of all ranks of British and Irish professional men met to know one another, to unite in the common cause of the advancement of knowledge, and to learn, on a great scale, how the mutual cultivation of science will efface national prejudices ; for it is only in this way that those national dislikes and distrustings which become hereditary feelings, transmitted from one generation to another, which separate peoples and delay the peaceful federation of the world, can ever be removed.

" I now respectfully and gratefully bid you farewell, and may all good things be yours."

The inaugural address by the new President, Sir Henry Acland, on the Medicine of Modern Times, was a faithful reflex of his own character and attainments.   Learned, refined, eloquent, and full of noble aspiration and philosophic thought, it fully justified the cordial acknowledgments that were given to the President at the end of the meeting, and the enthusiastic endorsement of Stokes' remarks in reference to his qualities as a man and a physician— qualities which had endeared him to all who knew him, and made them appreciate, as the speaker did, the gift of his friendship.

Seldom have nobler addresses been delivered than those on this memorable occasion. That on physiology by Professor Rolleston was a fitting inauguration of the work of the newly-formed Physiological Section. " An address at once so powerful and so charming," as was said of it by Professor Humphry.

The philosophic address on Medicine by Sir William (then Dr.) Gull, was listened to with rapt attention and mingled admiration and pleasure. It was, in truth, as Sir James Paget said of it, a " brilliant essay." Mention may also be made of the mirth-provoking discourse of Dr. Haughton, of Dublin, on the relation of food to force. This was found by the Association to be alike original and amusing.

In proposing a vote of thanks to Stokes for his services as President, Sir James Paget, who seconded the proposition which was proposed by Dr. Sibson, observed that he did so with what with some men were the strongest feelings of their nature—envy and regret. He had not been able to be present at the splendid meeting last year at Dublin, and be one of those who shared there in what he might call the jovial hospitality afforded to the Association. But he knew enough of the late President to say that in Counsel he was all that was moderate and wise; learned in science, upright as a man to men; and in social life genial and kind. In all these points the late president set those over whom he presided an example, and this example and the temper he had shown would dwell in the minds of the members for many years to come.

In the autumn of 1873 the writer delivered an inaugural address at the Royal College of Surgeons introductory to the Session 1873–4. Before doing so, he sent a short *précis* of it to Stokes, who was then in London enjoying a short holiday. The following letter was received in reference to the address :—

"GILBERT STREET, LONDON,
"*November* 2, 1873.

"MY DEAR WILL,—I feel that I should have been home before this and hope to reach Dublin on

Friday morning. I feel much better in many ways, and we have been very happy with Harriet and Griffith.[1]

"I like your programme of the lecture very much. That surgery has advanced medicine is true so far as it deals so largely with physical conditions, and it has been its safeguard against quackery, for no important surgical proceeding can be based upon it, at least, in the public mind. Still, it may be argued that medicine has even more advanced surgery, and the best surgeon is not the man who is the best operator, but rather he who knows best the laws of constitutional disease. I rather think that to the physiologist and pathologist are owing the development of physical diagnosis, the stethoscope, laryngoscope, ophthalmoscope, endoscope, galvanometer, sphygmograph, and so on. The progress of medicine has helped surgery and *vice versâ*.

"The shortcomings of the more modern school of so-called scientific medicine in the advance of chemistry and microscopic anatomy, are that its followers have become very vain, and in seeking to explain the laws of disease, dwell more on the physical than on the vital state, on the dead rather

[1] His daughter and son-in-law His Honour Judge Downes Griffith.

than the living organism. They thus neglect, or ignore the grand old records of medicine, and of surgery also, which belong to times when the microscope or animal chemistry were hardly known.

" As to hospitalism, by which I presume you mean the condition of bad health engendered in our wards, does it not greatly arise from want of ventilation and cleanliness ? I wish you saw the Radcliffe Infirmary at Oxford, in its worst state.

" Don't be afraid about your lecture. In reading it take care not to read too fast, and as much as you can, look your audience in the face. Love to dear Elizabeth.

" Ever yours,

" WILLIAM STOKES."

On March 17, 1874, William Stokes was nominated to the Presidency of the Royal Irish Academy. It was a new departure for the members of that body, which is mainly representative of literature and abstract science, to choose a physician as their head, but it was felt that the time had now come when medicine had attained such a position, through the labours of Stokes and others, in the estimation of literary and scientific men that the election of the

Regius Professor of that art in Trinity College
would be welcomed by the majority. It was remarked, besides, by the outgoing President, that he
possessed in a special degree one quality which was
sure to confer great benefit on any educational body,
namely, the power of imparting his own enthusiasm
in the pursuit of knowledge to those associated with
him in work, and that the Academy was sure to maintain its independence under such a guide. With him
the love of truth came first ; his native land and its
honour next, before every other consideration." In the
December of the same year, he delivered his Presi-
dential address before a crowded assembly. In this he
gave evidence of the truth of Dr. Ingram's remark as
to his special fitness for the place, " by the breadth of
views, and the respect for every form of useful intellectual effort, which so remarkably characterised him."
He takes in review the prospects of the body giving a
retrospective and prospective sketch of its career. He
enters into the questions of archæology, and polite
literature, and of science, and enlarges on the present
condition of the science of biology. The address
closes with these words :—

" The conservation of energy, directive though not
creative, in the living organised structure, and the

chemical affinities in that which is unorganised, show, it might be held, that a lower mode of life pervades every existing being; but we believe that in God's own time, that higher life which shows itself in progressive organisation, and is terminable, will have a different existence, at least, as regards the human being, one freed from material associations, freed from physical influences and from moral shortcomings.

"It is believed by thoughtful men that matter is indestructible. May we not find that as it has, in time, subserved the physical, so in Eternity it will, when spiritualised, subserve the moral law, and thus an undying result will be evolved.

"It has been written that we 'see as through a glass darkly;' but are there not grounds for the belief that such will not ever be the case? May we not believe that every discovery in development, in microscopical structure, in chemical composition, and in electrical and optical character, will be, when related to the property of life, a fuller ray of the burning lustre by which we approach the footstool of that throne where we shall be permitted nearer and nearer to contemplate the power and the ineffable light of Him from whom comes all life."

## XII

FAILING HEALTH—STATUE BY FOLEY—POWER AS
A TEACHER — PRUSSIAN ORDER, "POUR LE
MÉRITE"

FAILING health did not permit Stokes to hold
the Presidentship of the Academy for more
than two years from the date of the delivery of his
inaugural address, but in this space of time he guided
it through a period of no small difficulty and peril.
Those of its officers who were in constant communication with him at the time were deeply impressed by
his earnest zeal for the honour and welfare of their
body, and have borne testimony to the profound
interest often amounting to painful anxiety, with
which he followed everything which seemed likely
to affect its fortunes, and to the sound judgment
with which he early perceived what might safely be
accepted, and what ought never to be conceded.

In this year (1874) Stokes received the high distinc-

208

tion of the degree of LL.D. (*hon. causâ*) from the University of Cambridge. When the names are enumerated of those on whom this honour was conferred at the same time it will be seen that among the recipients were some of Stokes' most brilliant contemporaries. These were: Sir Alexander Cockburn, Bart., the Lord Chief Justice; Sir Bartle Frere, G.C.S.I., K.C.B.; Sir William Stirling Maxwell, Bart., M.P.; Sir Charles Lyell, Bart., F.R.S.; Sir James Paget, Bart., F.R.S.; Sir Garnet (now Viscount) Wolseley, G.C.M.G., K.C.B.; the Hon. Robert Winthrop; Sir George Gilbert Scott, R.A.; George Salmon, D.D.; Edward Freeman, M.A., D.C.L.; Nybain Leverrier; Joseph G. Greenwood; George Bentham, F.R.S.; William Lassell, F.R.S.; James Russell Lowell. In presenting Stokes for the Honorary Degree to the Chancellor of the University, the Public Orator, Professor Jebb, M.P., delivered the following speech : "Ut singulis locis, privatis domibus salutarem ac pœne maiorem quam est hominis opem potest afferre felix illa medicinæ ars, ita munus interdum sibi vindicat locorum spatiis universum, benevolentiæ complexu publicum. Sunt quædam communes sanitatis leges, quæ ut intelligantur non unius tantum foci, non regionis, sed populi totius interest. Perfecerunt huius viri labor, assiduitas, ingenium, doctrina ut quas vitales auras in ægroto hoc vel illo lenibus remediis faciliores facit, has totæ urbes, pestem vel patientes vel passuræ, veneno liberatas hauriant. Magnas unusquisque mortalium debet gratias ei qui lentæ illi pulmonum tabi succurrit ; ampliore tamen beneficio totum terrarum orbem is affecit, qui vicos, qui oppida, qui nationes pestilentiam propulsare docuit. Regium nuper Medicinæ Professorem, ne ceteros enumerem honores, Regii Professoris filium, et suo et patris et Academiæ Dubliniensis nomine jubemus— id quod ipse tot ægros iussit—salvere. Duco ad vos Wilelmum Stokes." [1]

At this time the statue of Stokes, which now stands in the hall of the College of Physicians, was executed by Foley. This artist himself thought it one of his best portrait statues, and would say, " I think I have caught the expression of the mouth, it was no easy task, to give that mouth ! "

Of this statue it has been well observed that the work is the expression in marble of a spirit, mournful indeed, but through thought and courage, serene. A spirit that has attained a massive wisdom and almost a

---

[1] Speeches delivered by the Public Orator in the Senate House, Cambridge, June 16, 1874.

gnomic calm, yet can be still enkindled from within and shake off the sense of the weight and mystery of life and death, of sin and sorrow that threatens to o'erwhelm it. With bowed head, and bending form, and folded hands, he is in the attitude of one who in utter stillness ponders intensely upon things unseen.

> " Believing that for every mystery
> For all the death, the darkness and the curse
> Of this dim universe
> Needs a solution full of love must be." [1]

At the unveiling of the statue (March 16, 1876), which ceremony was performed by His Grace the Duke of Leinster, and which was largely attended by many leading citizens of Dublin, distinguished members of the University and of the Royal College of Physicians and Surgeons, two remarkable speeches were delivered. One was that of Stokes' distinguished colleague and former pupil, Dr. Alfred Hudson, who, in a few well-chosen words, gave a brief but accurate epitome of Stokes' researches and professional work, and of how he had striven successfully to elevate the profession to which he had devoted his life's work.

Mr. Edward Hamilton, then President of the Royal College of Surgeons, also spoke on this

[1] See Poems by Archbishop Trench, p. 102. London, 1874.

occasion with his usual good feeling and warmth of heart. He observed :—

"I must give expression to the extreme gratification it affords me that the official position ·I occupy has given me the very great privilege of taking part in this interesting, pleasing, and, I would add, most important ceremony — pleasing, because we are called upon to do honour to a distinguished Irishman ; important, because I believe we this day commemorate a great and important epoch in Irish medicine. As the representative of your sister College, permit me to express an opinion, which I am sure is shared by every one throughout the length and breadth of the land, that Dr. Stokes is entitled to every honour which his professional brethren can bestow on him.

"He has lived amongst us a long life of stainless reputation ; he has been a skilled physician, a kind considerate friend ; he has worked with honest labour at the profession of his adoption ; he has endeavoured to promote her progress ; he has ever been the champion of her rights ; he has ever been the chivalrous guardian of her dignity and her honour. I think the proceedings of to-day have a far higher significance and a far deeper import than the honour we are doing to a distinguished individual. That marble statue will hand down to admiring posterity the features and form of one we loved so well; while it speaks to us of the honour conferred on him, which he so well deserves, it will also tell another story. It will remind us of the time when there was laid the foundation stone of clinical medicine in Ireland; it will remind us of the time when a work of progress was done; and although in past ages Ireland boasted of her school of physic, yet it was not until it was placed on the firm basis of bedside operation that it was able to take its position with the school in the sister country. Who was the pioneer in that work of progress? William Stokes. Therefore, I think that in unveiling this statue we commemorate an important era. When we have passed away like the grass that withers, and when our places know us no more, and when, no doubt, future ages, as they admire that statue, will ask, Who was William Stokes? I would say that not in the whole chaplet of honours that surrounds his name is there a brighter jewel than that which proclaims he was one of the founders of clinical medicine."

13

Probably one of the most generous and appreciative estimates of Stokes' powers as a teacher is one given by Dr. Arthur Wynne Foot, who for several years was his trusted and valued colleague in the Meath Hospital. Certain it is that there has been no one in recent years better qualified to form such an estimate, as all admit that as a brilliant lecturer, Dr. Foot proved himself not merely able to maintain, but also to enhance the great reputation of the Meath Hospital as a clinical centre ; a reputation made for it mainly by the efforts of Graves, Dease, Crampton, and Smyly, as well as by the subject of this memoir.

Dr. Foot emphasised the opinions of Stokes as to medical education when referring to a lecture delivered by him twelve years before, and he adds that he would even introduce a student who was ignorant of anatomy, physiology, and chemistry into the hospital wards from the first day he had made up his made to be a doctor, holding that anatomy, physiology, and chemistry are not the A B C of medicine. In this view, he adds, "I am supported by the opinion of our great master Stokes, who asks, in reference to these three branches of study, will they teach his hand, his eye, his ear ? But more, will they teach him the look of a sick man, sympathy with the sick, charity to the sick, patience with the sick? Will they soften his heart by witnessing their sufferings, or rejoice it by feeling their gratitude? No; and yet these things are of more importance to the moulding of his character and to his future usefulness than any knowledge of the accessory sciences, and he cannot begin to feel their blessed influence too soon."[1]

Another object which should be aimed at is suggestive, rather than exhaustive, teaching. On this subject I will quote again from a lecture of Stokes : "One word as to the duty of teachers, and this applies to those of other sciences as well as medicine. It is not to convey all the facts of a subject to their hearers, but it is, by precept and example, to teach them how to teach and guide themselves. If they succeed in this they have done their duty in the largest sense of the word." [2]

Another extract from one of Dr. Foot's lectures in Meath Hospital may be made as illustrative of the strong personal influence of Stokes. "As a teacher his sphere lay, of course, far above mine ; yet no one could come within the influence of

[1] Introd. Lecture, November 1, 1869.
[2] Stokes, " Med. Ethics," 1869, p. 5.

his presence and not be penetrated by a sense of the truth, earnestness, and reality which were ever manifest in his thoughts. . . . The object of his teaching was, not to fit the students for the examining boards, but to make them good practitioners. This result was ever in his view, and was the real cause of his incontestable pre-eminence in the wards, in the lecture theatre, and in his writings. It would be impossible to conceive a teacher less like what is popularly termed a 'grinder' than he was. Although a master of differential diagnosis in the right time and place, he did not draw the hard-and-fast lines between individual specimens of disease, so dear to the grinder and examiner.

"Tabular diagnostics, type diseases, positive assertions about pathognomonic signs, were not in accordance with his comprehensive and philosophic mind. He copied Nature, and Nature refuses to run like a canal in a regulated course within strict barriers. The life-long attachment of his pupils is the liveliest proof of his possession of all the qualities of a nature-made teacher. And why was it that we loved so much that grave, stern face, every line of which was marked with power, and before whose calm regard forwardness shrank back into the obscurity from which it ought never to have emerged, and the insanity of conceit became instantaneously sobered ? It was because we, who watched him closely, knew well that unfathomed seas of feeling lay beneath his composed exterior, and would from time to time break through, convincing us that the sympathetic man was the true man. It was because we saw that when the ear of the poor heard him, then it blessed him, and when the eye saw him it gave witness to him ; the blessing of him that was ready to perish came upon him, and he caused the widow's heart to sing for joy. It has been said that the inscription on Fichte's funeral obelisk might be rightly graven on the tomb of Stokes : 'The teachers shall shine as the brightness of the firmament.' Equally suitable, I would venture to suggest, would be the proud words of Hippocrates—''Ιατρός φιλόσοφος ισόθεος.' But why, it may be asked, do I now refer to Stokes, who, although in my own case, first a teacher, afterwards a colleague, and always a friend, has been seen but by few students of the present day, and whose ways and words are now matters of history in the archives of this hospital. It is because this is the first public occasion since his removal that I have had an opportunity for the expression of filial gratitude and reverential regard to his memory, and because his is a name which may fitly be invoked upon an occasion like the present, inasmuch as now he must be regarded as one of the chief makers of this hospital in which for nine and forty years he consecrated his genius to the service of the poor, in which he brought to light some of the profoundest truths of medicine, and from which he sent forth hundreds of sound and good practitioners, to whose exertions thousands, and more than thousands, owe their lives. . . ."

An obituary notice of Stokes appeared shortly after his death, by his friend and former pupil, Dr. J. W. Moore, and was published in the *Dublin Journal of Medical Science.* It is full of true appreciation and deep feeling, as the following passage attests :—

" A model and diligent student, he in time became a painstaking and successful teacher—the sympathising friend, the prudent counsellor, and the ardent well-wisher of every one of his 'fellow-students,' for so he called his pupils. But he was more than this. Those who have seen Dr. Stokes at the bedside of the sick know how gentle, how refined, how kindly was his bearing towards the patient. Amid all the ardour of clinical observation and research he never for one moment forgot the sufferer before him—no thoughtless word from his lips, no rough or unkind action ever ruffled the calm confidence reposed in him by those who sought his skill and care. In many eloquent lectures delivered in the Meath Hospital, he inculcated those Christian lessons of charity and thoughtfulness ; and so by precept and example he strove to teach the duties of a true and God-fearing physician."

" Dr. Stokes," says Professor Haughton, " when we are all passed away and forgotten, will be remembered as the advancer of medical science. He was profoundly convinced of the fact that medicine was not a science ; neither was physiology nor meteorology ; but he believed in his heart of hearts that medicine would one day become a science, and he felt that his task in life as a cultivator of medicine was to endeavour to take such steps, and to pursue such researches, as would help to elevate medicine from the empiricism of Hippocrates and the dogmatism of Galen to the position of an art which though not yet a science is about to become a science, and in order to convert the practice of medicine into a science he first established intelligent diagnosis, accuracy and precision in the distinction of diseases one from another as the basis of therapeutics. He laboured also to make the exact sciences the handmaid of practical medicine."

In the year 1876, and shortly after the unveiling of the statue in the Royal College of Physicians, he received a communication from Count Münster, the English Ambassador of the German Emperor, William I., presenting him with the Prussian Order " Pour le Mérite " of Frederick the Great, as a tribute in recognition of his contributions and original investigations in the science of medicine. The rare distinction had only been conferred on two Irishmen before, the late Humphry Lloyd, D.D., Provost of Trinity College, Dublin, and Dr. Romney Robinson, D.D., astronomer and scientist, and it may be regarded as the crowning honour of Stokes' life.[1]

[1] This order was originally granted only for military services in the field. In 1842, however, King Frederick William IV. extended the order, and granted it as well for proficiency in science and art. Among the " Ausländische Ritter " nominated in 1875 was " Wilhelm Stokes, Professor an der Universität zu Dublin."

St. Andrews Church

# XIII

## FINAL LITERARY WORK—LAST DAYS

T HE final literary work that Stokes undertook
was a biographical memoir of his lifelong friend
George Petrie,[1] "archæologist, painter, musician,
man of letters ; as such and for himself revered and
loved." The work was in every sense a labour of
love. In all matters connected with art and literature
there was a strong mutual sympathy between Petrie
and his biographer ; the former was through life, as
Stokes observed, "a rare example of purity and gentle-
ness of character almost feminine ; although when
called upon he could exhibit the greatest energy, firmness, and determination." Petrie's training as an

---

[1] "The Life and Labours in Art and Archæology of George Petrie,
LL.D., M.R.I.A., and Member of many learned Societies," by William
Stokes, M.D., D.C.L. Oxon, Physician to the Queen in Ireland, and
Regius Professor of Physic in Dublin University." London : Longmans,
Green and Co.

artist commenced in his earliest childhood under the guidance of his father, who was a portrait painter of considerable eminence. In connection with this artist an episode is introduced into Stokes' work that occurred during Petrie's childhood which is full of deep pathos : "Of the events of 1798, as well as those of 1803, Petrie preserved a lively recollection. His father, though a Loyalist, was yet on friendly terms with a number of the prominent political characters of the time, whose portraits he painted. Among them are Lord Edward Fitzgerald, Robert Emmett, John Philpot Curran and others—all most valuable from their truthfulness and excellent style of handling. After the execution of Emmett, he was requested to paint a portrait of him from memory, with the aid of such studies of the head and face as he had by him. It is needless to say from whom this order came. When the work was finished the artist wrote to Miss Curran, requesting her to come and see it. He was out when she called, but she entered his study notwithstanding. Petrie, then a little boy, was standing at the window concealed by the curtain, when he saw a lady, thickly veiled, enter and walk straight to the easel on which the work rested. She did not notice the child, and thought herself alone with the picture of her buried love.   She lifted her veil, stood long and in unbroken stillness gazing at the face; then suddenly turning, she moved with an unsteady step to another corner of the room, and bending forward, pressed her forehead against the wall, heaving deep sobs, her whole frame shaken with a storm of passionate grief. How long this agony lasted the boy could not tell, it appeared to him to be an hour, and then, with a sudden effort, she controlled herself, pulled down her veil, and as quickly and as silently left the room as she had come into it.   She was unaware of his presence, unconscious of the depths of silent sympathy she had awakened in the heart of the child, whose sensitive and delicate nature kept him from intruding on her grief."

Speaking of Petrie's love of the lower animals, Stokes says (p. 393)—

" There was, indeed, in him a full sympathy with the feelings so beautifully expressed in Coleridge—

> " ' He prayeth well, who loveth well
>    Both man and bird and beast.
> He prayeth best, who loveth best
>    All things, both great and small ;
> For the dear God who loveth us,
>    He made and loveth all.' "

As a landscape painter Petrie's work will be ever

prized for his delicacy, truthfulness, and refinement, and in music, his countrymen must be ever grateful to him for rescuing from an undeserved oblivion so many beautiful national melodies of Ireland, which are so much appreciated now by all true lovers of music.

On this subject he writes reproachfully : "The music of Ireland has been the exclusive property of the peasantry—the descendants of the ancient inhabitants of the country. The upper classes are a different race—a race which possess no national music, or if any, one essentially different from that of Ireland. They were insensible to its beauty, for it breathed not their feelings ; and they resigned it to those from whom they took everything else, because it was a jewel of whose worth they were ignorant. He, therefore, who would add to the stock of Irish melody must seek it, not in the halls of the great, but in the cabins of the poor. He must accept the frank hospitality of the peasant's humble hearth or follow him as he toils at his daily labours."

But that by which Petrie will chiefly be known to posterity is his work on the ancient architecture of Ireland, in which he finally established the Christian origin and ecclesiastical character of the Round Towers of the Irish monasteries, about the pagan origin of which there had hitherto been much discussion. When this work, the progress of which Stokes had persistently urged forward, was completed and laid on the table of the Royal Irish Academy, Petrie, thankful that his labour was at an end, and unwilling to be present on its presentation to the Academy, remained quietly at home. He describes in one of his letters to Lord Dunraven how at half-past nine he heard a loud rapping at his door. " It was Stokes, flushed with joy," who came to announce to his old friend the triumphant reception it had met with in the Academy. This work, the first that placed Irish archæology on a sound basis, was dedicated to William Stokes along with Edwin, third Earl of Dunraven, in the following beautiful letter [1]—

" MY LORD AND SIR,—You will remember that in one of the beautiful works of the great painter, Nicolo Poussin, he has depicted a group of shepherds at an ancient tomb, one of whom deciphers for the rest the simple inscription engraved upon it—

'Et ego in Arcadia,'

and it was a natural and grateful desire of the Arcadian

[1] See "Life of George Petrie," pp. 186, 209.

shepherd to be remembered in connection with the beloved region in which he had found tranquillity and enjoyment.

"In like manner I would wish to be remembered hereafter, less for what I have attempted to do, than as one who, in the pure and warm hearts of the best and most intellectual of his local contemporaries, had found and enjoyed a resting-place far superior to that of the Greek.

"As two of the dearest of those friends, equally known, beloved, and honoured by all, as by me, permit me then to inscribe your names on this humble monument, so that if it should haply survive the wreck of time, it may be known as that of one who, though but a feeble and unskilled labourer in the fields of art and literature, was not deemed unworthy of the warmest regards of such as you, and who was not ungrateful for his happiness."

The object of Stokes' memoir of his friend Petrie, was not merely to pay a deserved tribute to the memory of one who had been so gifted, and who had always been so loyal and steadfast a friend, but also to point out the importance of Petrie's labours in an educational point of view, and as establishing scientific methods of investigation in the study of archæology. It probably has also been of service in pointing out what, alas! is so little known in England, namely, the tone of feeling and the lofty aspiration which characterise the true Irish patriot.

After the memoir was completed Stokes received many appreciative letters from his literary friends congratulating him on the successful accomplishment of his task. Among them the following will be read with interest—

"FROM THE EARL OF DUNRAVEN TO WILLIAM STOKES.

"ADARE, *Dec.* 22, 1868.

"MY DEAR DR. STOKES,—Thanks for the delightful book which came this morning. I am very glad you did not write my name, as you will have to come and do it here, and the sooner the better.

"Do not trouble yourself about the omissions of your book. If the public is worthy of the work they can be inserted in due time. And in the mean time be content with having paid the noblest tribute that could be offered to your departed friend, and paid it so handsomely and satisfactorily. I really quite envy you—if such a feeling is allowable; as a friend I am truly proud of the result of your labours, and as Petrie's friend I warmly thank you for having with such truth, such feeling, and such thorough appreciation done honour to one of Ireland's most gifted heroes. You remember the old sign—'Rest and be thankful.' Apply that to yourself until the second edition is wanted.

" Yours,

" DUNRAVEN."

" FROM PROFESSOR HUXLEY TO WILLIAM STOKES.

" Jan. 13, 1870.

"DEAR DR STOKES,—I thank you very heartily for your letter, which has not only given me much pleasure but will be of great use to me. Of course I have never been a special student of Irish history but years ago I tried to make something of it in connection with my ethnological studies, and the general effect was, as the Germans say, ' like a mill-wheel in one's head.' I have had the opportunity more than once of examining the splendid collection of antiquities in the Irish Academy's museum, and I had a general notion of the great services Dr. Petrie had done to Irish archæology, but I was not aware that his work had the direct bearing upon Irish history which you tell me it has. I shall take the earliest opportunity of making myself acquainted with Dr. Petrie's writings and I beg leave to thank you in advance for the copy of his Life which you are so kind as to offer, and which I shall value all the more as it comes directly from yourself.

"It will be a great satisfaction to me if from what you and others have written to me I may permit myself to think that I have done something towards removing a prejudice which I believe has a very bad influence upon practical politics.

"Believe me, dear Dr. Stokes,

"Yours very sincerely,

"T. H. HUXLEY."

"FROM MR. J. LE FANU TO WILLIAM STOKES.

"18, MERRION SQUARE, S.

"*Jan.* 8, 1869.

"DEAR SIR,—Pray accept my very sincere thanks for the present of your memoir of our modest, beloved, and illustrious countryman, George Petrie, with whose acquaintance I was honoured and with whom it was impossible to have any acquaintance untinged by affection. His memory is happy in having found a biographer like you, who understood and loved not only his pursuits, but himself, with the high powers and sympathies to do so large a subject justice and with eminence to command attention.

    "Believe me, with much respect,

        "Yours truly,

           "J. S. LE FANU."

"FROM SIR JAMES CLARK, BART., PHYSICIAN TO THE QUEEN, TO WILLIAM STOKES.

      "BAGSHOT PARK, SURREY,

        "*January* 4, 1868.

"DEAR DR. STOKES,—I beg to thank you very sincerely for the volume which you have kindly sent me. I confess that it was not without surprise that I read your name upon the title-page as the author of such a body of print. It is true that when I glanced over it I found that the subject of it had written a large part of the volume. This arranging the matter and putting it altogether is no small work, and I am surprised that you could find time with your extensive practice and your many professional labours to compose that work. Petrie seems to have been an extraordinary man and writes well and strongly. . . .

"I am, dear Dr. Stokes,

"Sincerely yours,

"J. A. CLARK."

It has already been pointed out that Stokes possessed an exceptional power as a relater of anecdote. This was doubtless due to his dramatic instinct, to his intense interest in every form of human character, and to his wide and deep sympathies with the sorrows, as well as the joys of all those with whom he came in contact. He combined, as Sir Henry Acland has said, "real delight in all intellectual development with the deepest sympathy for the suffering. Nothing could equal the pathos of his voice and utterance when telling a tale of sorrow and suffering among his countrymen, or the keen sense of humour he displayed in the relation of many of his experiences acquired in all classes of society throughout the length and breadth of the country. Some of these anecdotes may be recorded here, although it is mainly from memory that the writer ventures to repeat them :—

Father Burke, an aged priest, and Dean of Westport, related the following story illustrating the deep religious feeling of the Irish peasantry. "I had the largest parish in the diocese though I was the Dean, and had no less than four curates—God help them. They were scattered here and there through the mountains. It was a Sunday morning early, and you never saw such heavy rain as was falling, when a boy on a horse rode up to my house with word that Father Sheehy was taken very bad, and would not be able to celebrate Mass. All the curates had their hands full. I was going to breakfast, but I had to go off without it, and the rain was so thick and heavy that in five minutes I felt the water running down my back as it poured in through the roof and sides of the covered car in which I was travelling. Well, I went on, the blast and the storm only seemed to increase as I got higher and higher among the mountains for the best part of twelve miles, when the boy pulled up. 'What are you stopping for?' said I. 'For your reverence to say Mass,' said he. 'Where?' said I. 'There,' he said, pointing with his whip to the ditch, where I saw a large white flagstone. 'That's the altar,' he said. So I got out and put on my wet vestments, and after a while one poor creature came out of the mist and then another, and then a woman and a man carrying their child, and then more and more, till a great crowd gathered round the stone, so great that you could not see the end of it in the fog and mist ; and they were all wet to the skin after walking over the mountains in the storm, and then all of them, on their bended knees, when I came to the Elevation of the Host, called out with one voice, 'Céad míle fáilthe, Chriost mo shláinte!' ('A hundred thousand welcomes ! Christ my salvation ! ')"

Enough has not been said of Stokes' unostentatious charity, his friendship for the poor—and none felt this more than the poor of Howth. There was a cobbler living near Carrig Breacc who was in broken health for many years. He was fond of reading, and Stokes lent him an odd volume of Scott's novels from time to time. Walking beside him one day on the road Stokes said, "Well, Denny, what did you think of the last book I lent you?" "It's a great book intirely, docther, an' Sir Walter Scott's a true historian." "I'm inclined to agree with you," said Stokes ! " but what do you mean exactly by calling him a true historian ?"

"I mane, your honour, he's a thruc historian, because he makes you love your kind."

Stokes always spoke of this afterwards as one of the finest comments he had ever heard on Scott. It would be vain to attempt to describe the sympathy for the poor and suffering which he could throw into his voice as he told such a tale as the following incident in his hospital practice, which is of interest as seeming to show the power of the will in prolonging life. An old pensioner, a patient of Stokes' in the Meath Hospital, whose life was despaired of, and whose death was hourly expected, was one morning distressed and disappointed at observing that Stokes, who, believing that the man was unconscious at the time, and that it was useless to attempt anything further, as his condition was hopeless, was passing by his bed. The patient cried out in an agonised tone of voice, " Don't pass me by, your honour, you must keep me alive for four days." " We will keep you as long as we can, my poor fellow," answered Stokes ; " but why for four days particularly ? " " Because," said the other, " my pension will be due then, and I want the money for my wife and children ; don't give me anything to sleep, for if I sleep I'll die." On the third day after this, to the amazement of Stokes and all the class, the patient was still breathing. The students then began to lay wagers among themselves as to whether he would survive for another day and become entitled to the pension. On the morning of the fourth day he was found still breathing and quite conscious, and on Stokes coming into the ward he saw the patient holding the certificate which required signature in his hand. On Stokes approaching him the dying man gasped out, " Sign, sign ! " This was done, and the man sank back exhausted, and in a few minutes after crossed both hands over his breast and said, " The Lord have mercy on my soul," and then passed quietly away.

Shortly after his wife's death, a sorrow from which Stokes never recovered, a fall from a car, while on a professional visit to the County Wicklow, was followed by symptoms of spinal concussion, which appeared to be the determining cause of the development of the paralytic affection which gradually weakened his perceptive faculties, and ultimately deprived him of the power of his limbs. He also felt much the further narrowing of his family circle by the death of his daughter Janet [1] and the marriage of his daughter Elizabeth.[2] The progress of the failure in his intellectual and physical powers were very slow, a deep sleep apparently falling on him, from which for long he in vain strove to rouse himself.

[1] Wife of Mr. (afterwards Sir Henry Edward) Stokes, M.C.S.
[2] Wife of the late Mr. John Boxwell, Commissioner of Dacca, I.C.S.

At times he would do so and be then as intellectually clear and brilliant as ever. But these periods, like gleams of sunshine that at times suddenly flash from dark clouds that presage a storm, were brief and seldom recurring. His family then urged him to give up all work, and to resign the Presidency of the Royal Irish Academy and his seat on the General Medical Council. It can well be imagined what a severe wrench it was for him to have to take these necessary steps, as it had always been a fixed resolve of his to "die in harness," as he himself said, and he could not divest himself of the idea that to yield was cowardly. At length, however, he consented, and resigning all public work, went to end his days at his residence at Howth, where the beauty of the surroundings filled his exhausted spirit with thankfulness and peace. The writer has a vivid recollection of the day when his father relinquished all work, and sadly left his old home and the city, in the public life of which, for more than half a century, he had taken so prominent and distinguished a part. Seeing him slowly and reluctantly driving away, never to return, vividly recalled to his mind Turner's masterpiece of the old Téméraire going to its last resting-place.

At Carrig Breacc, his beloved retreat at Howth,

away from all disturbing influences, he spent the last days of his useful life with his daughter Margaret, solaced by the presence, sympathy, and care of those nearest and dearest to him, and the frequent visits of many of his best friends, among whom may be mentioned Dr. Jellett, the late Provost of Trinity College, the late Rev. Dr. Russell, President of Maynooth College, Sir Samuel and Lady Ferguson, Dr. Ingram, Professor Mahaffy, Lord Justice Fitzgibbon, Dr. Gordon, Dr. H. Fitzgibbon, Dr. A. W. Foot, Dr. J. W. Moore. These and others used to go down to see him, cheering him by their presence, and bringing him tidings of what was going on in the outer world. He spent his time chiefly in reading the works of Shakespeare, Scott, Trench, Tennyson, and the Arthurian Legends, in which latter he took the keenest interest. The poetry of Burns, Shelley, Byron, and his friend Sir Samuel Ferguson, were never-failing sources of keen enjoyment. Music, ballad poetry, his plantations and flower garden, and observing the beautiful and ever-changing effects of mist and cloud, sunshine and shadow on the bay beneath him, and the fair Wicklow hills beyond, were all sources of deep delight.

But the time came when all such interests ceased;

for early in November, 1877, he was struck down by a sudden paralytic seizure from which he never quite rallied, though he lingered on for two months after this. He grew steadily weaker, and on January 6th, the Feast of the Epiphany, he quietly, and apparently without suffering, passed into his long rest " to where beyond these voices there is peace."

It was his wish, and that of his family, that the funeral should be private, and this was communicated to the academical bodies and learned societies to which he belonged. But it was not found possible, so that although these societies were not, so to say, officially represented, a large number of distinguished persons connected with them attended, and made it virtually representative. From the Meath Hospital, so long the arena of his professional labours and scientific achievements, and the two Royal Colleges of Physicians and Surgeons, came a long procession of mourners. The country people, most of whom had come the day before, laden with flowers, to take a last look at the face of their friend, now petitioned that they might carry the remains from Carrig Breacc to the Church of St. Fintan—the " grassy churchyard grave " on the western slope of the Hill of Howth, where he was to be laid beside his beloved wife and children.

# LAST DAYS

The morning was clear and summer-like as they bore him tenderly to his last resting-place. A mist lay over the churchyard, but just as the procession reached the gate this cleared off and showed the picturesque ivy-clad ruins of the ancient church, at the western door of which he was to be laid. Here a stalwart band of devoted and true-hearted students from his hospital begged to be permitted to carry their beloved master for the rest of the way to the grave—the teacher on whose lips, now closed for ever, they had so often hung, enthralled alike by his earnestness, enthusiasm, and eloquence, and ever eager not to lose even one of the golden grains of knowledge of which he was so prodigal. They laid him in the same grave and beneath the same stone with her who was the beloved companion of his life, and on whose tomb he had engraved those words :

> "When the ear heard her, then it blessed her,
> When the eye saw her it rejoiced,
> When the poor and suffering came unto her
> They were comforted."

> "Awake him not, surely he takes his fill
> Of deep and liquid rest forgetful of all ill."

# APPENDIX

# APPENDIX

BIBLIOGRAPHY

*Dr. Stokes's Works.*

1825. "A Treatise on the Use of the Stethoscope."
1828. Two Lectures on the Application of the Stethoscope.
1837. "Diseases of the Chest."
1854. "Diseases of the Heart and Aorta."
1868. "Life and Labours in Art and Archæology of George Petrie."
1874. Lectures on Fever.

*Articles in "Dublin Journal of Medical Science" by Dr. Stokes.*

May, 1832—January, 1872.

"Clinical Observations on the Exhibition of Opium in Large Doses, in certain Cases of Disease," i. 125.
"Contributions to Thoracic Pathology," ii. 51.
"Contributions to Thoracic Pathology," iii. 50.
"Researches on the Diagnosis of Pericarditis," iv. 29.
"Researches on the Diagnosis and Pathology of Aneurism," v. 400.
"Researches on Laennec's Vesicular Emphysema, with

observations on Paralysis of the Intercostal Muscles and Diaphragm, considered a new source of Diagnosis," ix. 27.

"Researches on the State of the Heart, and the use of Wine in Typhus Fever," xv. 1.

"Researches on the Pathology and Diagnosis of Cancers of the Lung and Mediastinum," xxi. 206.

"Observations on the Case of the late Abraham Colles, M.D.," i. 303.

"Observations on some cases of Permanently Slow Pulse," ii. 73.

"On the Mortality of Medical Practitioners from Fever in Ireland" (Stokes and J. W. Cusack, M.D.), iv. 134.

"On the Mortality of Medical Practitioners in Ireland," second article (Stokes and J. W. Cusack, M.D.), v. 111.

"Clinical Researches on the Gangrene of the Lung," ix. 1.

"On the Prevention of Pitting of the Face in Confluent Small-pox," xxix. 111.

"On some Requirements in Clinical Teaching in Dublin," li. 38.

"Some Notes on the Treatment of Small-pox," liii. 9.

*Papers read to Societies by Dr. Stokes, reported in "Dublin Journal of Medical Science."*

August, 1835—February, 1874.

"On the Diagnosis of some Diseases of the Thorax," viii. 196.

"Softening the Heart with Thinning of its Parietes," xxi. 133.

"Bright's Disease of the Kidney," xxi. 144.

"Acute Induration of the Lung," xxi. 151.

"Cirrhosis of the Lung," xxi. 293.

"Gangrene of the Lung," xxi. 317.

# APPENDIX

"Aneurism of the Abdominal Aorta, opening into the Parenchyma of the Lungs," xxiii. 166.

"Vegetation on the Semilunar Valves, causing Patency," xxiv. 279.

"Atrophy of the Heart in Phthisis," xxiv. 283.

"Granular Kidney—Diabetes—Pneumonia—Hydro-thorax," xxiv. 295.

"Observations on Dr. Bigger's Communications at the last Meeting (Contraction of Left Auriculo-ventricular Opening)," xxv. 526.

"Fatty Degeneration of the Heart," i. 491.

"Hypertrophy with Dilatation of the Left Ventricle, in an Anæmic Subject," i. 493.

"Aneurism of the Arch of the Aorta, compressing the Œsophagus, and perforating its Parietes," i. 498.

"Jaundice—Fungous Growth round the Orifice of the Ductus Choledochus ; Dilatation of the Hepatic Ducts in the Liver," ii. 505.

"Aneurism of the Abdominal Aorta, involving the Cœliac Axis, bursting by a large rent into the Peritoneum ; gradual Separation of the Serous Coat from the Liver and Stomach by Aneurism ; Absence of Caries of Vertebræ," ii. 519.

"Hydrocephalus," ii. 526.

"Encephaloid Tumours in the Abdomen," x. 202.

"Psoas Abscess bursting into the Cavity of the Peritoneum," x. 471.

"Endocarditis : Disease of the Mitral Valve," xi. 198.

"Aneurism of the Thoracic Aorta," xi. 201.

"Partial Displacement of the Sternal End of each Clavicle," xiii. 459.

"Aneurism of the Abdominal Aorta," xv. 480.

"Diphtheria," xxxv. 175.

"Cancer of the Liver," xxxviii. 201.

"Pelvic Abscess," xxxviii. 440.

"Stricture of the Pylorus," xxxviii. 448.

"Cancer of the Gall Bladder," xxxix. 218.

"Report on Three Cases which occurred in the Meath Hospital under the care of Drs. Stokes and Hudson," xliv. 193.

"Disease of the Aortic Valves," xliv. 423.

"Cancer of the Liver," xliv. 428.

"Chronic Ulcer of Stomach, opening the Coronary Artery," xlv. 201.

"Cancer of the Thyroid Gland and Adjoining Lymphatics," xlvi. 220.

"Pulmonary Phthisis, with Emphysema," xlvii. 216.

"Ulcer of the Stomach," xlvii. 220.

"Heart in Typhoid Fever," l. 197.

"Phlebitis of the Cerebral Sinuses—Disease of the Tympanum," l. 212.

"Cancer of the Stomach and Mesentery," l. 220.

"Varicose Aneurism," lii. 249.

"Cancerous Tumours of the Abdomen and Thorax," liv. 67.

"Chronic Inflammation of the Spinal Chord and its Membranes ; Disease of the Spleen," lvi. 62.

"Enteric Fever," lvii. 483.

"Enteric Fever ; Intestinal Hæmorrhage," lviii. 97.

*Short Report on a Case by Dr. Stokes in "Dublin Journal of Medical Science."*

"Observations on the Existence of a Proper Fibrous Tunic of the Lung," vi. 471.

*Articles in " Cyclopædia of Medicine."*

1832–33.

On Derivatives, Dysphagia, Enteritis, Gastritis, Gastroenteritis, Inflammation of the Liver, and Peritonitis.

# APPENDIX

*Lectures published in the " London Medical and Surgical Journal."*

## 1833.

" On Theory and Practice of Medicine," delivered in the Meath Hospital and Park Street School of Medicine, vols iii., iv., v., vi.

*Lectures published in " Medical Times and Gazette."*

## 1854.

On Fever.

### *Addresses by Dr. Stokes.*

1854. Discourse on the Life and Works of Dr. R. J. Graves.

„     Opening Address of the Medical Session T.C.D., on State Medicine.

1861. Address on Medical Education.

1864. Address on Medical Education (second).

„     Address on Life and Works of Mr. Josiah Smyly.

1865. Address in Medicine before the British Medical Association, Leamington.

1867. Inaugural Address as President of the British Medical Association.

1868. Valedictory Address before the British Medical Association, Oxford.

1874. Address as President of the Royal Irish Academy.

### *Papers by Dr. Stokes.*

1832. " On the Curability of Phthisis Pulmonalis."

1842. A review of Kugler's Hand-book of Painting.

1850. " On Mesmerism."

# DEATH OF THE POET CLARENCE MANGAN.

## LETTER FROM THOMAS O'REILLY, M.D.,
## ST. LOUIS, MO., TO THE AUTHOR.

*March 8th,* 1898.

MY DEAR SIR WILLIAM,—Nothing could give me more pleasure than the receipt of your letter of the 22nd ulto., as I entertain the most grateful recollection of your father's kindness to me, a poor young man striving to advance in life, without acquaintances, and without money. I feel indebted to him for whatever of good fortune has befallen me, and naturally, I would be an ingrate if I were not the friend of your family, therefore you can understand my delight on hearing from you.

The note in your Memoir in reference to the death of Clarence Mangan in the Meath Hospital is mainly correct, except that it was I (not the porter) who drew your father's attention to him. He was shivering and almost naked when he presented himself for admission, but I had him cleaned and put to bed in the public ward as I would have done with the ordinary patients. His miserable condition did not impress me, as the applicants for hospital admission at that time were almost all destitute, but what did impress me was the amazement of your father on seeing him. For a moment he seemed bewildered, as if he did not recognise Mangan, but it was only for a moment, as he told the class the patient before them was Clarence Mangan the poet. Your father, with his characteristic humanity and sympathy, turned to me and directed that Mangan should be placed in a private room, clothed with flannels, and supplied with every necessary comfort at his expense. I think the poor fellow lived only eight or nine days after his admission, and I am almost certain your father paid his funeral expenses through Mr. Parker the hospital steward. The account of the artist is also correct, except an omission. The head was shaved and a plaster cast of the head and neck was taken. I saw it a few days after in the house now occupied by you. Some five or six years ago I wrote to Sir Charles Gavin Duffy, then at Nice, correcting a statement by him, to the effect that Father Meehan paid Mangan's expenses. He acknowledged the receipt of my letter and promised to correct this statement in the next edition which he was about to publish, but as I never saw the new edition, I cannot say that he fulfilled his promise. Will you kindly put me down for a copy of the Memoir on your father?

And believe me to be your grateful friend,

THOMAS O'REILLY.

# INDEX

# INDEX

## H

Hamilton, Sir William Rowan, 78

Hamilton, Mr. Edward, 211

Hatchell, Dr., 107

Haughton, Professor, 202, 219

Heart and Aorta, work on Diseases of, 133–44

"Home Rule," 106

Hospital, *see* Meath Hospital

Hudson, Dr. Alfred, 68, 125, 211

Huxley, Professor, 228

## I

Ingram, Dr., 206, 237

Irish Academy, the Royal, Presidency of, 205, 236

Irish Church, disestablishment of, 100

## J

Journals, contributions to, 50, 51, 62, 133, 182

## L

Laennec, 33, 51, 64, 65, 66, 69, 71

Lecky, Mr., *note* 25

Letters, from Wales, 38; Dublin, 43, 44, 61, 102, 103, 104, 114; Ballinteer, 47; Brussels, 53; Tyrol, 56; Co. Mayo, 59, 60; St. Go-thard, 74; Helen Faucit, 82; on art, 85; from the Rhine, 95, 96; Co. Sligo, 118, 120; Nice, 150; Dresden, 154; London, 152; Letterfrack, 190; South of Ireland, 191; London, 203; Earl of Dunraven, 227; Professor Huxley, 228; Mr. Le Fanu, 229; Sir James Clark, Bart., 230

Liver, inflammation of, 62

*London Medical and Surgical Journal*, contributions to, 50

## M

McCullagh, Professor, 79

MacNamara, Dr., 59, 60

Madonna di San Sisto, 154

Magee, Archbishop, 26

Mahaffy, Professor, 84, 87, 88, 237

Mangan, Clarence, 78

Marriage, 47

Meath Hospital, 30, 34, 38, 39, 40, 42, 45, 50, 64, 158, 173, 178, 180, 214, 215, 219, 234, 238

M.D. (*hon. causâ*), 72

Medicine, Regius Professor of, 20, 99

Medicine, School of, Dublin 40

# INDEX

# INDEX

UNWIN BROTHERS, THE GRESHAM PRESS, WOKING AND LONDON.

www.ingramcontent.com/pod-product-compliance
Lightning Source LLC
Chambersburg PA
CBHW031425020726
47499CB00005B/1600